PENGUIN BOOKS

DEATH AND THE MAIDEN

Apinuch Petcharapiracht is an author and a chef. She is the co-founder of Ladys & Moonscape Books. She was born into and raised in a family of Chinese descent in Thailand. She has published twelve books across a wide variety of genres. She is known as a writer with a distinct style and a morbid passion for gothic romance. She lives in Phetchaburi with a black cat and a dog named Cocoa.

Death and the Maiden

Apinuch Petcharapiracht
Translated by Pimpida Pitaksonggram
and Danaya Olarikded

PENGUIN BOOKS
An imprint of Penguin Random House

PENGUIN BOOKS

USA | Canada | UK | Ireland | Australia
New Zealand | India | South Africa | China | Southeast Asia

Penguin Books is part of the Penguin Random House group of companies
whose addresses can be found at global.penguinrandomhouse.com

Published by Penguin Random House SEA Pte Ltd
9, Changi South Street 3, Level 08-01,
Singapore 486361

First published in Penguin Books by Penguin Random House SEA 2024

10 9 8 7 6 5 4 3 2 1

This is a work of fiction. Names, characters, places and incidents are either the product of the author's imagination or are used fictitiously, and any resemblance to any actual person, living or dead, events or locales is entirely coincidental.

ISBN 9789815144710

Typeset in Garamond by MAP Systems, Bengaluru, India

www.penguin.sg

Contents

Prologue

In our tower, whichever floor that is, somebody is plastering the wall.

I can feel it. It is like how I am aware of the black rain that seeps through the ceiling. The droplets fall into the potted plant that I have been raising. New green leaves are sprouting from the small ornamental plant whose name I do not know. Each branch pokes through the ribs buried in the earth, resembling the bronchi that spread within the lungs and around the heart. I look up at the rows of clay pots above—they are also full of flowers. Among the colourful blooms, I am only familiar with the little hogweeds, a species that seems to grow anywhere and everywhere. Their name, which anyone can recall, really suits their pig-headedness. If I were the me that I used to be, I would have been able to name more than a thousand types of plants. Someone used to tell me while stroking my hair, 'Sweet child. You have a green thumb. You can grow anything . . .' I don't exactly agree with the title of 'sweet child', since that is not me at all. The latter part is true, though. I really do have a green thumb. That is why everywhere I go, the plants are all very happy.

Where I live right now is the dressing room of the theatre on the eleventh floor of a high-rise tower. This tower was abandoned even before it was completed. It has become *our* domain. I am in-charge of keeping the eleventh floor clean and tidy, which is why I sometimes have to bring myself to run up and down and keep my relationships with the others going. The Gamblers on the floors above like me. Aunties and uncles seem especially delighted when they see me at the window where they fall past every evening. A group of lost children on the floors below keep following me around. I do not like kids. You can even say that I hate them. Even though my age is not that of an adult and I have lived through almost the same number of years as them, I do not consider myself one of them. It is even more annoying when they stop before the theatre doors and keep pestering me to allow them inside. Once they get in, they refuse to let go of my limbs. One time, they even pulled off the ribbon that Vikal had tied for me. It flew down into the bushes beside the building, and there was no way for me to retrieve it.

'Twinkle, twinkle, Little Star . . .'

Holding each other's hands, they form a circle and start to sing.

'How I wonder what you are . . .'

'Shut up!' I yell. They smirk, elbowing each other in the hips. Perfect timing, as always. They all show up not long after the sun sets, their irritating giggles and laughter echoing all over the tower's nooks and crannies. Crossing my legs on the shiny padded chair, I ask them the same old question.

'What do you guys want?'

'Twinkle, twinkle, Little Star . . . Parva Stella, tell us a story.'

'Why do I have to tell a story to brats like you?'

'Because the new girl won't stop crying.'

The group parts down the middle, revealing an unfamiliar little girl who's sobbing and rubbing her eyes. I look at the group of eight useless noisy children, boys and girls aged between five to ten years. They remind me of the Lost Ones from *Peter Pan.* The two eldest boys had appointed themselves as leaders and have been fighting for the role of Peter Pan. Since there can only be one Peter Pan, I think they look more like Ralph and Jack from *Lord of the Flies*, who never see eye to eye. The most annoying thing is how these imps keep multiplying and now it is only getting worse.

'Are you the newcomer?'

I crouch down beside her and try to ask her name. She keeps shaking her head like people do when they are confused. The girl looks to be about seven years old and is wearing an expensive-looking dress—that has already become dirty—with a cartoon princess on it. Her face is covered with tears. The girl has been crying so much that her skin is starting to bruise.

'All right, stop crying. Which story would you like to hear?'

'Bean Princess,' a girl says and is immediately booed by the group's leader.

When I make a disapproving sound, he interrupts with, 'I want the King with the Donkey's Ears.'

'I've told you that donkey king story a million times.'

'But I want it!' the boy screeches. The rest of them start to disagree.

'I'm tired of the donkey king. I want Baba Yaga.'

'No. The one about the dancing corpse in the woods is way better,' a short kid declares.

'No way. It's too scary,' a kid with glasses says. He glances at the newcomer's dress and mutters, 'Hey kid, is that the Little Mermaid?'

The newcomer stops crying and nods quickly. We are all relieved. At least now we know that she has something of a favourite. The act of consolation won't be as difficult anymore.

'Then, Stella, tell us the story of the Little Mermaid,' they conclude.

'Hmph. All right.' I drop myself onto the quilted armchair and rest my chin on one hand, posing as the female protagonist among all the extras. 'Have any of you been to the sea?'

Amid the group of kids on the theatre's floor, some raise their hands, saying that they have, and some merely say no. Most of the time, their answers are 'no' or 'can't remember'. They are too young to remember the world in their own way, yet they know stories from every corner of it.

'What does the sea look like, Stella?' a tall boy asks with a curious tilt of his head.

'There's a lot of water there,' a boy with freckles cuts in. 'Stella's told us before.'

'How much?'

'A lot, a lot,' the same boy says, spreading his arms wide.

'Shut up. I'm asking Stella, not you.'

I look at the newcomer and ask, 'Do you know that at the edge of the land, there is a vast body of water?'

The girl and the Lost Ones run around, all saying that they do not know.

'The water body at the edge of the land is called the sea. Humans have only explored one-twentieth of it. There're still so many oceans that they haven't been to. Like the Milk Sea, the Blood Sea, the Perpetual Still Water, the Bone Sea—'

'What's the Bone Sea?'

'It's the graveyard of the sea people. Their last resting place when their lifespan is over.'

'Have you ever been to the sea graveyard, Stella?'

'No.'

'Why not?'

'If you keep asking about something unrelated, I won't tell the story anymore.' I tip my chin up. 'The reason why I haven't been there is the same as why you lot don't get to be in heaven. Because you're brats.'

'Then you're just like us,' the leader of the group talks back. 'You're a brat too.'

'Just stop,' Leader Number Two says. 'We're getting nowhere with the Little Mermaid because of you.'

I pretend not to care about them, turning back to the newcomer and continuing.

'In the land of a vast water body called the sea, there live the sea people. They're without souls. Their bodies turn to sea foam and become one with the sea graveyard when they die. Except when they're in love. A requited one.'

'Ew!' One of the girls makes a face.

'This is the story of a little mermaid who falls in love with a human—'

'A beautiful mermaid, right, Stella?'

'Yes, she's a beautiful mermaid. Her hair glows like stars, her eyes are the same colour as the sea.'

The beautiful mermaid with long, lovely hair has been living her beautiful life. Until that one fateful night, when everything changes . . .

'Please continue, Stella.'

I close my eyes and images appear behind my eyelids. Above our tower, a sperm whale is dashing through the sky, calling out to other whales in deep frequencies.

'Mmm.'

The sound of someone plastering the wall has quietened down. Outside the tower, the wind is bringing forth the smell of grief from the capital city along with its evening bustle. Nocturnal birds on the power lines are chittering, relaying some important news. It seems like there's a wildfire in the north, heavy rain in the south (the soil is getting healthier again), and a flood in the north-east. The world keeps on turning and there's nothing that we can do about it. We cannot save anyone. 'Poor them, poor them, poor them,' they harmonize. The story about a mermaid goes on.

'Scylla is a shoal, Charybdis is a whirlpool.' I try to make my voice solemn and respectable, but the new girl will not stop sobbing. I have witnessed this same scene so many times that I've become used to it. All the newcomers always cry their eyes out on their first day.

It is only normal.

Who wouldn't cry when they realize that they are dead?

1

'Blackbird'

It takes a long time for the newcomer to finally stop crying. The girl forces herself to press her wobbling lips into a straight line, the skin around her eyes so swollen and deeply bruised that it looks purple. After a while, a kid around eight or so, steps up to her and offers her a hand. She grabs that small pale hand and follows him into the group of kids around her age. These kids almost always look emotionless. They all smile and laugh at the same time as if there is a start and stop button. They only cry on the first day of their arrival. After that, their youthful eyes turn into empty crystal balls. They forget everything, including their grief and all of their memories. But they remain as stubborn as children are. They're innocent, heartless, and will never grow up.

That is one of the reasons I never consider myself to be one of them.

We are not the same.

I watch the kids run out of the theatre and then walk around to check if those brats have caused any damage to the furniture that I had arranged in order. I stroke the padded armchairs, talk to the ancient doorframe, shake the dust out of the curtains, and admire the neat stacks of sheet music on Vikal's desk. This place has become much lovelier ever since Vikal brought me here.

I still remember the first day of my arrival. We stopped in the dark in front of the gold-plated wooden baroque staircase. The red carpet was all torn up. On the bare wall hung two signs—'To the theatre' and 'Caution: uneven surface'. Every grain of dust was asleep on that silent night.

'This used to be the prettiest floor once,' Vikal said in a hoarse, toneless voice. 'A long, long time ago.'

How long ago was that? I wonder. I could not imagine how many years it would take to transform the colourful angels on the stained-glass ceiling into a canvas of someone's nightmare. All the seats inside the theatre had been removed, leaving only an empty stage at the end of the slope. The fine teal velvet curtains had fallen off the hook and lay crumpled on the ground. The overall atmosphere had been blanketed in horrifying darkness. I lit the first, the second and the third candle with a match that I kept on my person. The theatre started to welcome its visitors little by little, as well as the furniture within it that multiplied as time went by.

I stand on the stairs, all distracted, and a second later, he is there at the door. Even without footsteps, I become aware of his presence. He scrunches up his nose, sniffing something with suspicion in his eyes.

'Who did you let in?' He asks as soon as I open the door for him.

'The kids,' I reply. 'If you don't like that, I won't let them in again.'

'Do whatever you want,' he says tersely. He takes his coat off, hanging it on the bone hanger on the wall, and walks around the place with distrust. Turning to me again, he asks, 'No outsiders?'

'No way. Who'd wanna visit this haunted tower?'

'It's happened before,' he mutters. 'The living.'

'Nuh-uh.' I rest my chin on one hand. 'Are you afraid?'

He pretends not to hear the last question. I let out a sigh, disappointed that I don't get to see him wearing any other kind of expression—raising his voice, making a scene, or exhaling in exhaustion. My attempts to stir him up yield the same effect as throwing sticks into a bottomless sea.

I hug my knees and watch him do the most mundane things. Retying his ponytail at the back of his head into a loose bun; changing from shoes to slippers. Then he turns to me, rubbing his chin, thinking, 'The ribbon?'

'Lost,' I drawl.

'Ah.'

There's no anger in his voice, a fact that makes me feel incredibly guilty for responding in such a heartless way. It's still something that he got for me because I was the one who asked for it—like that high-quality lace dress from France, the deep red Mary Janes made from veal leather, the long Gypsy head scarf sewn with shiny sequins, the Swiss hand-winding pocket watch, tens of baby-doll shoes in the closet, along with all the furniture that makes our lives a lot easier without me having to set foot outside the eleventh floor.

He stops behind me. I can feel his cold, calloused hands, trying to get rid of all the knots in my hair, followed by the touch of the oval wooden comb massaging my scalp. This is a job that requires patience. I don't even want to do it myself. I close my eyes, groaning softly like a lazy kitten. This person is too admirable. Never angry. Never complains either. His kindness eventually gets the best of me and prompts me to confess.

'Those kids pulled it off,' I say. 'The ribbon.'

'Mhmm,' he makes a sound in his throat, indifferent.

'It probably fell onto the ground floor. If you allow me, I'll go and bring it back.'

'No,' he replies. 'It's late.'

'Tomorrow morning, then.'

'No,' he repeats. 'I'll go get it for you.'

'Hmph. I knew you'd say that.'

I look up and into his eyes. A famous man once said, 'Staring into beauty is no different from staring Death in the eye'.

I disagree. The very first time I met Death, he was not that beautiful to me. I grew up in a swamp of ugliness and witnessed as much selfishness as a small child could possibly experience. I would see that even more if I came with him, he said, before grabbing my hand and pulling me out of the hollow of a tree. At the time, his tall figure reminded me of a black cuckoo, a thought that gave me the feeling of being a bad omen. His black and navy coat, shiny and strangely patterned, was designed to broaden his shoulders. On his face was a chilly expression. To sum it up, he felt so repulsive that I wanted to turn my face away from him.

But that's him. That's Death.

'Sorry for being difficult. I really can't help myself when I see you.' I stare Death in the eye and beam. 'Welcome home, Vikal.'

He is still expressionless, but he leans forward to kiss the back of my hand, and then, in a soft whisper against my skin, he says, 'I am back.'

2

'Scene by the Brook'

'Vikal.'

'Mhmm.'

'Do people still have to work after death?'

'Not everyone does,' he replies. 'But being a Messenger of Death is one such profession.'

'What do you get in return?'

'Nothing.'

'Then, it's for nothing,' I say.

'For nothing.' He nods.

His name is Vikal. That black cuckoo. That Messenger of Death.

I tell him that while I was still alive, I had never seen a Messenger before. He raises an eyebrow, surprised, then says that there are indeed many of them; that I can see them everywhere. I ask him how many and he tells me that no one really knows, but that I must have seen them more than once before.

'Do you see that flock of nocturnal birds?' He points to the black cloud cruising merrily across the orange evening sky. I squint. They seem like a group of noisy sesame seeds, chattering away in the distance.

'Of course.'

'Those are Messengers.'

I quirk an eyebrow. 'Are all nocturnal birds Messengers of Death?'

'Only the flocks that fly in a backward V formation.'

'Never knew that they are social creatures.'

'Cholera, wars, accidents—with all the deaths, only one Messenger is simply not enough.'

'What about the ones that fly alone?'

'You'll never know if it's an actual bird or one of them until—'

'Until you're dead.'

'*Almost* dead,' he corrects. 'Sometimes they appear before it's time. As an omen.'

'What for? Mental preparation?'

Vikal shakes his head.

'Because sometimes the Messengers are biased. Just like humans.'

Vikal sounds impassive, like a stream flowing through the pasture in the country. It doesn't save an insect from a toad, nor does it reject a dead rat swept in from the fields. His voice is low and unpleasant. I can never read between his lines and he never tries to clarify any of them. We live together, the ambiguity acting as our boundary. I reserve the dressing room as my private space while Vikal usually stays in the abandoned storeroom for musical instruments. He doesn't come into my room, but I always go into his whenever I want to clean it.

Vikal tells me that I can decorate our theatre as I wish, as long as I make sure not to be seen by the living or stumble outside of the tower, and that if there's anything I want, he'll get it for me. With that kind of opening, I initially meant to be as difficult as possible. My list of necessities only consists of ornaments and fineries that I would never have been able to get my fingers on when I was alive. He tries his best to look for those items for me. Whenever he comes home, he looks no different than a greedy, black bird carrying shiny trinkets in its beak. An incredibly funny image every time.

I start to decorate this place as I used to do in human society. Clothes arranged neatly in the closet, I learn to make some furniture—racks, poles for vines, candlesticks—materials for which I gather from within the tower. I'm lucky that the neighbours quite adore my face because the Gamblers on the upper floors are all so eager to give me their *old parts*. They take me to some floor above the thirtieth and open the bathroom door to proudly show me a completely intact human skeleton hanging from a noose connected to one of the wooden beams.

'Can I really take it?' I repeat for the third time.

'Sure, sure,' the old man insists. 'It's been here for twenty years and no one's found it yet.'

The auntie puts one hand on her hip, looking scandalized; she pinches her nose even though she can't be affected by the smell.

'Disgusting. My dear Stella, promise me you'll wash your hands thoroughly.'

'Of course,' I reply like a good kid.

Other than the skeleton, I will not describe anything else in the bathroom. You can imagine how a body that's been hanging in a dark room for twenty whole years without being properly buried would look. It takes me a lot of effort to break it into parts then scrub each and every single one of them clean—all while the kids from the lower floors run around me ceaselessly. The leader steals the old man's pelvis bone and hides it. Four Eyes asks me for the leg. I allow them to have what I don't use for their personal collections.

When Vikal comes back, despite finding me in such a filthy state, he doesn't say anything. I made bone racks for hats and coats as a gift for him. He doesn't smile at or praise me, but I know that he likes them because he's been using them every day since.

In our free time, we help each other arrange the living room that's never been used to welcome any guests. After dragging the round tea table onto the faux fur carpet, we decorate it with a bowl of red and white grapes along with comfortable padded chairs suitable for reading. I ask Vikal to find me a lot of books every time he goes out and, much to my amazement, he's able to get me every single one of them. Although they are old, they have been well-repaired and are in such great condition. I once asked him where he procures these books from. He said that shops also exist for people in the twilight world like us.

'Really? I wanna go outside, too.'

At first, I thought he would reply right away that it was impossible, but this time, he hesitated.

Then he said, 'When there's a chance, I'll take you there.'

3

'Flight of the Bumblebee'

Vikal is always busy after the sunset.

'While humans die all the time, the Messengers work in shifts,' he tells me.

Vikal tends to cut the story short when he has to talk about someone else. Chin on my hand, I've been watching him getting dressed since half past five. He's wearing that same ugly black coat with a navy pattern, the one that makes him look like a black cuckoo. He ties his hair up into a tight ponytail, and then lifts the hood up to cover the upper part of his face. Combining that with the shoulder pads, he turns into a giant walking shadow. I can only let out a disappointed sigh when I look at him.

'What?' Vikal raises an eyebrow.

'Why do you have to dress like that? You look quite handsome when you're at home.'

I smile cheekily like the kids on the floors below. Vikal pretends he didn't hear it and adjusts his belt. I get up from the sofa and follow him out of the theatre.

'Where are you going?' He clears his throat, voice hoarse and low.

'I'm walking you there.'

'No need.'

He's panicking. I can sense it from the way his tone becomes flat at the end. That excites me even more. 'I'll only go down to the ground floor. No one's gonna see me, isn't that right?' Tilting my head, I feign innocence. 'I'll go look for the ribbon.'

'Forget the ribbon.'

'Don't say that about my precious possession.'

Vikal, who is trying his best to hide his unease, does not realize that he is waking the bad habits that I've been trying to keep in check for a long time. A bit more. A bit more and he'll show his true emotions. I walk past him down the stairs and he quickly follows after me. The further down we go, the faster I get, taking two steps at a time toward the end.

'Stella!'

A voice calls me from the west, where the orange sun is disappearing behind the buildings. I am met with a familiar sight of the middle-aged Gambler who's falling past us from above. I remember her. She's the auntie who adores my face. I quickly yank the robe of the Messenger next to me.

'Look, Vikal, we're just in time for the parade.'

When he turns around, that body has already hit the ground, shattering. I can hear the kids running merrily around the remains, laughing, 'HAHAHA, a fallen star! HAHAHA, a star has fallen onto the ground!' They whistle and sing 'Twinkle, Twinkle, Little Star' while holding hands and going in a circle.

Twinkle, twinkle, Little Star,
How I wonder what you are,
Up above the world so high,
Like a diamond in the sky,
Twinkle, twinkle, Little Star,
How I wonder what you are . . .

The kids' high and low pitches harmonize with the sounds of something falling: *whoosh–thud–whoosh–thud–whoosh–thud* as the Gamblers on the top floor line up and take turns dropping themselves to the ground. Each of them greets me warmly when they see me. 'Good evening, Stella.'

'Good evening, Gambler.' I give them a curtsy, but they fall too quickly to see it.

'Good evening,' the next young man greets me while tipping his hat.

'Good evening to you, too.' I smile at him.

The first time I saw this parade, I was so terrified, I almost peed my pants. I was sitting with the other kids on the ground floor, telling a story about the broom closet witch as Four Eyes had requested. Suddenly, I heard the sound of something hitting the solid ground next to me. A round eyeball fell out of its socket and bounced to where I was, staining the pretty dress that Vikal had gotten for me.

'Somebody jumped off the building!' I screeched.

Seeing me frightened, the kids roared with laughter while pulling me out of the courtyard and away from the parade's trajectory. When I looked up, there were dozens of people lining up on the top floor. The first one jumped, then a minute later, the next one followed. Not long after, the courtyard was full of their broken bodies.

'Twinkle, twinkle, Little Star. Parva Stella, you're such a fool. What are you scared of?'

'I'm not.' I covered my mouth with one hand, feeling like vomiting, and used the other one to bonk the kid's head.

'It's all right. They do this every day,' a girl said. 'They clean up after themselves, too. We don't have to help them.'

'We call them the Defeated Gamblers.'

'I heard that they lost a lot of money or something. What word did that uncle use again?' I asked.

Four Eyes replied, 'Bankruptcy.'

'Wot's a *bankwupchy*?' A five-year-old slurred out the question.

One of the leaders answered, 'It's when your bank gets ruptured, you stupid boy.'

'It's not like that,' I objected. 'It means you owe someone so much money that you can never pay it off.' Everyone looked up at me, gaping with admiration when I said that.

'So that's why they have to jump off the building,' the boy continued.

'I think so, too. They only say, "It's hopeless now" and jump.'

'And die!' the youngest one yelled.

'Yes, they jump and die like that every day.'

'If they do that, will they be able to pay off their debts?'

'They're dead. They don't have to pay it anymore,' the leader said. 'But I heard it was their duty to jump every day.'

'It's their routine!'

'Who decided that?' I asked. No one had an answer.

'If someone screams or is scared of them, they're a little bit happier.'

'Once they're done here, they'll go back up and continue with their gambling. I used to go up there and listen to what they talked about.'

'What did they talk about?'

'Hmph!' The kid shook his head. 'It was gibberish. Boring.'

They all burst into laughter, before walking around in circles until their shadows on the walls were like those of the devils. The memory layers itself onto the image in front of me. Everything is almost the same, except for the fact that Vikal and I are still up here in the tower. The parade starts and stops at the same time every day.

'It's over.'

I cross my arms and turn to Vikal.

'That means I'm about to be late for work,' Vikal says, glancing at the children below with disdain. 'In such bad taste. They don't respect their elders at all.'

'I agree. If those brats were still alive, I'd really love to see one of the leaders get squashed by a falling body. That auntie jumped from the forty-seventh floor, right? Vikal, I once learned that if a human falls onto a car from a high enough place, even its hard metal could get bent. Now imagine if it was a human being.'

'I don't wanna say this, but you're no better than them.'

'Just say it then,' I challenge him. 'You-are-a-bad-kid-you-are-disrespectful-you-will-go-to-hell.'

Vikal doesn't answer, his lips pressed into a straight line. He flicks his robe and leaves with the last bit of twilight. I look at the back that seems bigger than it actually is and laugh because I know he would never berate me like that. No matter how despicable I become, even if I am like one of those wretched imps from the floors below, even if I sneak out of the tower when he's away and mingle with the living, he would merely find me and bring me back here quietly. He would wipe the dirt from my clothes and comb my tousled white hair and tame the scatter of black strands—like he does every morning when he comes home.

I cannot say how I know this. I just do. Like how I'm aware of the black rain that seeps through the ceiling; of the fact that once a month or every two months, someone from 'the living world' will sneak into our tower, taking advantage of the terrible silence, and plaster the walls on one of the floors.

4

'Pathetique'

Time in the tower full of death stands completely still. The only movement seems to come from the hands of the manually wound watch that stubbornly ticks away every second. Other than that, all of the shadows around the tower are occupied by the blurry forms of every spirit that still lingers from the past. I used to think that I was a part of this place, just like the Lost Ones or the Defeated Gamblers, until one day, change seeped in as if a string quartet was playing a piece so slow and sweet, and suddenly a high-pitched woodwind entered in the middle, turning it into a jazzy tune that requires great improvization skills to be brought to the end.

It all begins in the middle of the rainy season. You may have already realized this, since every bad thing in this world always happens in the middle of the rainy season.

The first drop of rain falls around three in the afternoon, followed by the heavy rain that pours non-stop until six in the evening, changing the capital city into the city of water. I am no longer surprised by the high-rise buildings that the living now tend to favour everywhere, because if the rain continues like this for three more days, the first floor of every building will be submerged. This idea rushes through my head as I sit spaced out on the padded chair inside the dressing room. The rumbling sky and the pitter-patter of the black rain quietens the chaos in my head. I eventually fall asleep under the black-and-white thunderbolts that are tearing through the sky.

Vikal quietly slips out to go to work. He is always one with the darkness of the theatre. Once he wants to vanish, he does it without leaving a trace. I only go in and tidy up his room when he is not around. I gather all the scattered pieces of sheet music one by one and put them into separate stacks with cardboards between them: Chopin's *Nocturne*, Schubert's *Rosamunde*, Beethoven's *Violin Sonatas*. His messy scrawl on the sheets feels gentle and aloof; a mere reflection of himself. I admire him and feel mad at him at the same time, because he's never let me listen to any of his practice sessions, not even once.

I blow out the candles in the musical instruments' storeroom and light up the chandelier in front of the stage. The plant in the bone pot raises its splendid violet flowers towards the light. I kiss the small bud, softly begging it to bloom as fast as the others. As I bend down to water them, the doors to the theatre spring open. The leaders and their little followers all dart right at me, each of them pulling at my limbs from every direction.

'Twinkle, twinkle, Little Star.'

'Stella, let's go and play.'

'No.' I turn my face. 'Go away.'

'Let's go and play,' Lanky repeats.

'Play what?'

'Let's go to the sea!'

'Fool. There's no sea in the middle of the city!'

'There is. Like what Stella told us, the sea is where there's a lot of water.'

I look down at the kids with disdain and let them walk down the stairs into the darkness below, only to find out that the ground floor of this tower has turned into a swamp. The stench of the clogged sewer that has not been maintained for years permeates the air. Garbage bobs up and down in the water. I look around and frown.

'It's like the Little Mermaid that Stella told us about.'

This is like the Little Mermaid? I am about to quip, when I turn around and see their dreamy faces. Not wanting to spoil their excitement, I announce, 'Fine. This is the sea.' The dirty floor is the beach, the insects scuttering away from the water are tiny ghost crabs and restless hermit crabs, and the tower is the lighthouse. The children hold hands in a circle, all of them pushing and pulling me toward the edge of the sidewalk, easily crossing the sacred border that Vikal has forbidden me from.

'It's dangerous. What are you doing?' I scowl at them. Not answering, they glance at each other, mysterious smiles on their faces, and wait until there's a bronze car coming our way. We are bathed in bright headlights and a huge black wave. My favourite skirt is dripping with sewage water again, and my hair that Vikal has combed so neatly is now a mess. 'You're really pushing your luck, you little imps,' I hiss, raising both arms up like a monster in a bedtime story. The kids scream and shriek with laughter until I can't help but follow along. We roll around in the shallow water under a utility pole, the kids flapping their arms as if doing a backstroke.

'Stella.' Four Eyes points at the bulk of intertwined electrical wires weighing down the slanting pole. 'Will we be electrocuted if this pole falls?'

'Aww, stupid,' I say. 'You're already dead.'

'Yes,' the new girl says. The eyes that used to be so swollen from all the crying are now dry. They seem more like crystal balls now. 'We're all dead.' She speaks the brutal truth like it's none of her business.

'I think we were lucky that we didn't die by electrocution,' adds the sickly child. 'It'd hurt so much.'

'Yup. We were so lucky we didn't die of old age or live long enough to suffer from painful diseases before dying,' says the girl.

'Or until we couldn't move and became bedridden.'

'Lucky we didn't go bankrupt and jump off a building.'

'Or get hit by a car.'

'But we were murdered,' Four Eyes says.

He's looking up at the evening sky, eyes distant and unseeing. It's at that moment that I sense the shift in the atmosphere. The chatter has disappeared. The sea is no more. We are still lying in the shallow swamp and I absent-mindedly watch the glittering stars from the nearby street. Hundreds of people walk past our wrought iron fence without noticing any of the strange children playing in the puddles.

Four Eyes continues, 'We died in so much pain. That man killed us.'

I used to wonder about this, but I never asked anyone. It seems like now is a good opportunity.

'What does your killer look like?'

The Lost Ones, who are never afraid of anyone, tremble with fear. They all talk at the same time, but this is the gist of it: 'He was a big guy and seemed very kind'; 'He smelled a bit. His room, too'; 'He invited me to play games and gave me snacks when I was crying because I got lost and couldn't find my mom'; 'He said that mom was coming to take me home later.'

I listen to them. 'And then what?'

'He tried to do something to me. He told me he would teach me how to play a game, telling me to sit on his lap, but I didn't want to. I said I wanted to go home.'

'That's why he stabbed me with a knife.'

'Yes.'

The kids stand up and start to act out the scenes.

'He dragged me across the floor.'

'He stuffed me in a sack.'

'And locked us up somewhere in this tower.'

'Next to me.'

'And to me.'

'With the others that he killed.'

I frown. 'And no one caught him?'

'No one,' the kids answer. 'That's why there's always more of us.'

'That man deserves to die,' I remark, feeling a sting deep in my chest when I think about their living families. The parents of the Lost Ones are still looking for them, not knowing that they're not there anymore.

Our high-rise tower is located in the middle of the business district of the capital city. The wrought iron gate has never been locked. Once in a while, tourists will sneak in, going up to the top floor to take photos of the view. The city from up there is beautiful; you can see the city's major river cutting through it. If they come in the evening hours, the Defeated Gamblers will give them a warm welcome at the entrance with the jumping parade. Shocked by the gruesome scene, some tourists would get so scared, they would call the police. I would watch them with the Lost Ones, giggling among each other, when the police would come and not find anything. The police stopped coming eventually. Even so, I have never seen any of the kids' parents come here and search for their bodies.

You may have noticed that I do not extend my sympathy or well wishes to the dead. Their stories have ended and will go on in a loop of the past, like the Gamblers who cannot accept their fate or the Lost Ones who will forever remain children. Their crystal eyeballs are full of innocence, no guilt, no growth, no heart. But the living are different. Limitless possibilities lie ahead of them. It is sad to be held back by the past.

'The living won't come back here a second time,' I mutter to myself.

Except for one man.

The man who keeps plastering the walls of whichever floor that is.

5

'Partita'

By the time we get back to the tower, it is already daybreak. The white moon, chipped and pale, is floating in the sky above the skyscrapers. The sea of darkness is receding. At a time like this, when the light is dim, I usually see the past overlapping with the present.

Two girls in dresses run around in the colourful dream world of the living, away from the sunlight. The tiled floor alternates between the purging cassia yellow and Sacramento green. The longing scent of summer. The stench of salt. The stink of sweat on damp clothes. The aroma of ripe fruits. The saccharine sweet vanilla ice cream on red jelly. Strangers walk, stand, sit, and sleep everywhere. The place where the girls grew up, they see the things they're doing as taboo—skipping school, sneaking out during the sacred ritual, reading forbidden books during breaks, yelling and raising their voices. 'Wretches like you will be punished by Heaven,' Father scolds them in public. 'You have no right to enter the Holy Land. But since you were born here, Hell despises you, too. You must wander this sinful path until the Day of Judgement, no different from Adam's eldest son.'

Vikal stares at me when he gets home. I stare back at him with a cheeky smile.

'You left the tower,' he accuses.

I raise an eyebrow. This is unexpected. I thought that the very first thing he would say would be, 'Why are you so dirty? Where have you been?' And I was ready to reply cheerfully with, 'The dirty swamp on the ground floor.' But no, he doesn't bring up my clothes at all. I don't understand how Vikal knows about things that are out of his sight. (Not to mention the fact that despite being a Messenger, he still needs to wear glasses because of his short-sightedness.) I conclude that it may be the hunch of a supernatural being like him. When he points at the bright yellow allamanda in the vase on the round table, I can't help but laugh. Of course, we don't have yellow allamanda in our tower.

'Yes, I went out.' I tilt my head, testing him. 'Are you going to scold me?'

'No.' He pushes his glasses up. 'You're back.'

'Don't wanna hear about it?'

'No.'

'I saw the living.'

Vikal quirks an eyebrow. I rest my chin on the padded armrest and start describing the things he didn't ask about.

'I went out at night, past the wrought iron gate that's never been closed, past the homeless man who was sitting on flattened cardboard boxes to keep himself dry in the rain. The road near the tower was full of bright lights and car fumes. I jumped around, pretending I was evading bombs on the sidewalk. The last step was a miss. The dirty rainwater from under a loose tile splashed at a woman behind me, making her scream, "Holy smokes!"'

'And that flower?' Vikal points at the flower behind my ear, its colour is the same as the one in the vase.

'Got it from an old lady with puffy hair. She reached out towards me when I was walking past her around the corner of one building. I started a little when I realized she could see me. The old woman was sitting there with a magnifying glass and tarot cards. Her face was all wrinkly and her smile was quite scary.

When I looked closer, I noticed that her lips were very dry, so I told her that I would fetch her some water. I looked at the brightly lit convenience stores in the area and saw many people lining up to the cashier. But, you know, I didn't have any money to pay for anything, even though it was right in front of me. I thought that they wouldn't mind if one small bottle of water disappeared, so I borrowed one. Don't make that face. The old lady was so happy she finally got a drink.'

Vikal takes off his robe, hanging it on the bone rack. He narrows his eyes and says nothing.

'Speaking of which, I'm kinda thirsty. Maybe some tea would do,' I complain.

'Wait a moment,' he replies.

We sit down, facing each other, the round table between us, and drink foreign tea with big green grapes under the chandelier's candlelight. It's funny when Vikal fidgets because he cannot help but please me. I know those eyes very well. They tell me that there are so many things he wants to ask, but since he does not say anything, I keep going on with my own story.

'I crouched down and asked the old lady how I could keep up with the news. She said the Internet or television. I didn't understand the first word, so I asked where I could watch TV for free. She told me that there were no such things these days. Nothing's free anymore. Then she stared at me. Her eyes were clouded like people with glaucoma. She grinned and said that she knew what I was looking for. And then she handed me something.' I swing my legs back and forth while telling the story and look up at my listener. 'Do you find it strange, Vikal, that a stranger knows I'm looking for something, when the man next to me doesn't?'

Vikal's eyes soften. It occurs to him now that I've been trying to squeeze the questions out of him. 'Fine.' His glasses reflect the candles' flames. 'What were you looking for out there?'

'The murderer,' I reply flatly.

'There are plenty of them in the capital.'

'I only want one.'

I retrieve a piece of paper from my sleeve. Unfolded, it reveals a photo of a girl, probably around seven, with double braids and a bright expression. She's the latest member of the Lost Ones, the girl who likes Little Mermaid. On the paper, it is written in big bold letters: 'MISSING'. Vikal's eyes dilate a little, a shift so minute only I can notice it. Vikal has never paid the Lost Ones any attention before, and he tends to stay away from the other occupants of the tower as much as he can. The Lost Ones are also afraid of him. If there is anything in this world that those little rascals are terrified of, it is either the Messengers or the murderer who took their lives.

'There's a phone number here.' I point at the text below. 'Her parents must be worried sick. I think we should—'

Vikal snatches the paper from my hand and tears it up. It falls in small pieces to the floor.

'Are you kidding me?' His voice is hoarse and low. I know he's trying to control his emotions. 'You'll bring *the living* here.'

'I haven't told you what I wanna do,' I grin. 'Have you ever heard that if a person expects the worst, God will grant him the worst?'

'You just appropriated the Bible.'

'Yup,' I laugh.

Vikal massages between his eyebrows wearily. I am actually impressed that he hasn't snapped yet, despite my best efforts to the contrary. A moment later, he puts his hand down and looks me in the eyes. 'Listen,' he repeats the message that he's said more than a hundred times before. 'Death has its own rule, and that is "Don't interfere." If someone is getting murdered, we have to let it happen.'

'Let the evil-doer still do evil, and the filthy still be filthy, and the righteous still do right, and the holy still be holy . . .'

I sweetly recite a verse from the Bible to annoy him. Vikal looks the other way and unties his hair, letting the long black tresses fall onto his shoulders. He looks a lot slimmer when he's not wearing that ridiculous robe. I swear I'll burn the hideous thing one day.

'Do as you please. Good day,' he says and walks back to his room.

'What?' I bite into an apple with a heavy heart. *What is it today?* Why was he so brusque?

The morning sunlight is shining in the world of the living. It's time to sleep for the ones who live after sundown. Vikal disappears into the instrument storage room. The melody of a solo violin partita floats into the air.

I sit listening.

6

'The Flower Duet'

Fingerboard, pegbox, scroll, F-holes, bridge, tailpiece, chinrest, bow.

The violin is a small musical instrument, yet so painfully complicated. I'm not only talking about its parts. Its sweet and high-pitched sound, like a widow's cries created by a human's touch, is even worse. I used to believe that it was an abominable invention since I learned that from the place I grew up in. The instrument is shamefully shaped like a naked woman's curves. A harlot sitting on a wild beast, embellished with gold, jewels, and pearls. In her hand, she holds a cup full of foulness from intercourse. The kind of woman who wears a short, revealing skirt, showing off her long, slender legs. The legs that dance along with the music at a party, and the very same legs that spread for a great many men. Our Father told us this story with his face contorted in disdain. He kept repeating the importance of virginity, the purity that would keep us away from any sexually transmitted diseases. For him, the violin was the agent of plagues and death.

I also wonder why it has to be the violin, since there are thousands of other musical instruments in this world. Why only brand one particular instrument as a mark of lechery? I once told Father that I had read about the Pied Piper of Hamelin, who lured all the kids in the city to follow him to their death—why was a pipe not included in this category? It ended with me having to write down verses from the Bible the whole night as a punishment. It was not because I doubted him, but because I read a book from outside. Father always saw them as evil and nonsensical. My close friend climbed up to my window that night with candied apples and vegetable crackers that her mother had made, along with a green carnation and another one of the forbidden books.

'I don't regret for a single moment having lived for pleasure. I did it to the full, as one should do everything that one does. There was no pleasure I did not experience. I threw the pearl of my soul into a cup of wine. I went down the primrose path to the sound of flutes. I lived on honeycomb . . .' she read, her tone going up and down as I copied the verses from the Book of Isaiah. '. . . Religion does not help me. The faith that others give to what is unseen, I give to what one can touch, and look at.'

'Such blatant insults toward God, this perverted writer!' I mocked, although I'd been listening to what she was reading.

She shrugged and asked if God were the reason I was being locked up, would I not blame Him even a little?

'Have you never dreamed of a life full of roses, sweet and lush as a honeycomb? Are you really satisfied with being a foolish little lamb and will you do what Father says until you rot and die? If that's the case, then I think I'm visiting the wrong person.'

'Shut up. You looked so pleased when Father decided to punish me.'

'We all agree with what Father says, my friend,' the girl lorded over me. 'Only a fool would argue with him. Only a fool would rise up, act like his enemy, and in return not receive any food as well as have to write down verses all night. If you were a little bit wiser and acted a little bit more sweetly, everything would go smoothly. And one day, we'll escape this place together.'

I had never agreed with her idea. She always put on a flattering smile and fawned over Father until she was allowed to sit on his lap at the dining table and received the softest portion of the meat—along with dolls, lavish stationery sets, and the bed right next to the window, as requested. Yet, even though we bickered every day, we both shared the same goal. The one and only goal—running away from there.

I finally achieved that goal, although it wasn't the way I'd planned. The day I left that place, I realized that Father's assumption toward the violin was not entirely wrong when I heard that slow tune coming from a place far, far away—on the same night I was destined to die inside the hollow of a tree and meet Death for the first time. Death stood big and tall in a black robe with navy streaks. He was tilting his head to the side, round glasses reflecting the red, fiery blaze, a brown wooden musical instrument tucked between his chin and shoulder. The piece sounded sweet and sorrowful, and reminded me of a widow's cries. Mozart's 'Requiem'.

The Messenger plays the violin to lull his passenger who walks the path to the other side. Neither for entertainment nor to show off. No matter how many times he plays it for those hungry spirits who are stuck here in this world, it is a waste of time. Vikal hasn't said that to my face, but I can read it in his body language. He always stops playing every time he sees me nearby. After the night we argued, I started to do more things behind his back. Since he said that I could do as I pleased, it is not my fault at all if I find his private documents when I'm cleaning his room and read through the list of people who are going to die soon. There is a name whose date has been crossed out and rewritten many times in red ink. The first time it appeared was last year, the second time was two months ago, and the latest record states that it'll be here next week. It's a simple name, consisting of only four letters.

Maya.

'Who's Maya?' I ask him.

'That doesn't concern you.' Vikal seems clearly irritated that I'm being nosy, I deduce from the way his pupils grow a millimetre wider. Still, he doesn't scold me and merely glances at the folder with the list. It seems like I will never find his important documents on his desk ever again. I step closer and repeat the question. 'Who's Maya?'

'Someone who's going to die soon,' Vikal replies, annoyed. 'A woman who wouldn't die as scheduled. Even though the date's already been set twice.'

'Can people even do that?'

This time, Vikal falls silent, as if holding his tongue. He doesn't want me to poke my nose into his job any more than I already do and is probably searching for a way to handle me. Instead of letting him achieve that, however, I use my wiles to strike first and corner him, causing him to be at an apparent disadvantage—starting with asking him to comb my hair. He loves the pale grey curls on my head too much to refuse and never wants to pass this task on to any of the Gamblers who are constantly asking to do it for their dearly beloved Stella. When he gets to bury his fingers into my thick locks while brushing them with the bone comb, the stress in his muscles eases. For faster results, I move onto the second strategy immediately.

'You're exhausted from work. Do you wanna listen to some music?'

'What are you up to this time?' Vikal pauses, suspicious.

I giggle and then softly hum 'As the Deer'. 'As the deer panteth for the water, so my soul longeth after Thee . . .' He knows I'm endearing myself to him for the secrets, but he's always had a soft spot for me. Like how the Gamblers adore my face and how the Lost Ones keep begging me for stories to soothe their sorrow. Once I reach 'You're my friend and You are my brother, even though You are a King,' Vikal finally gives in and promises to tell me about the girl who refuses Death.

'Maya is an orphan,' Vikal begins the story of a stranger whom he knows from work, and then skips right to talking about her decadent life. She worked as a nude model while having a heated relationship with a middle-aged man she'd met at a bar. He was a dangerous man who was involved in great many horrible dealings at the same time. She only loved him, but he shared her love with the friends in his wicked circle. Curiosity killed the cat, and Maya became too deeply entwined to escape. Once the man realized that she was trying to resist, he intended to get rid of her. He's planned to kill her twice already.

'But the girl named Maya has also survived twice, according to the list.' I nibble on the grapes while listening to him. 'You let her get away.'

'That's a very severe accusation,' he notes, implying that it's not true. 'Death has its own way. The Messengers do not interfere when people are killing one another—it'll do them more harm than good.'

'But Vikal wants her to survive.' I smile. He turns his glance away and that's all the confirmation I need. 'You've been following her for a while now, since you have to send her soul away. But when you see her fighting spirit and how it has helped her escape Death twice, you can't help but root for the poor girl. She is to die unjustly. You want her to survive. Am I right?'

Vikal goes quiet.

I push him some more. 'How will she die next week?'

'One bullet through the heart,' Vikal answers. 'We're not gonna talk about this again. Please, don't push me too hard. You know I can't do anything but watch.'

'But I'm not the Messenger.'

Raising my head, I stare into his trembling eyes and whisper something he never expects to hear from a tiny spirit he's taken in.

'Rely on me.'

7

'Devil's Trill'

I thought that Maya was a woman with the kind of beauty that would make even the Messenger's tears fall when she died. When I see her in real life, she's a bit different from what I had in mind. Our female protagonist in this act is quite short, with a figure flat and straight enough to be mistaken for a boy's. Her hands are round, her fingers plump and her limbs so thin, they look as if they could turn 360 degrees. What I find most interesting are her slanted, stray-cat eyes under thick-rimmed glasses and her agility when she hops around the place. I stand behind her while she queues up to enter the art gallery on the day that is destined to end with her death.

Vikal should be around here somewhere, keeping watch after dropping me off. The morning I offered him my help along with the details of what I could do for him, he neither agreed nor refused. He merely gazed into my eyes, his own wavering. The whole day thereafter, he kept repeating the rule that Messengers could not interfere with the death of human beings, no matter how terrible they may be, along with his work ethic that forced him to remain indifferent. Not unlike a documentary cameraman who doesn't stop a lion from darting at a boar even though he's secretly rooting for the poor animal. I laughed and waited.

When the fateful day came, he knocked on the dressing room door and adjusted that speckled robe as if he was inviting me out.

'The Messengers do not appear outside of their working hours. You have to go in alone,' he said and raised his fingers, one by one, as he repeated the rules. 'Don't stand out. Don't talk to the living. Don't look into the living's eyes, not even Maya's. Do you understand?'

I asked, 'Who's supposed to be her killer?'

'The dangerous man that she's involved herself with.'

'And who's that?'

'You'll see.'

'When will it happen? What's the hour? The minute? The second?'

'I can't tell you.'

I scoffed. He narrowed his eyes. He must have felt very sorry for that girl, enough that he was willing to pin his fleeting hopes on the kid whom he'd never let out of the tower before. The way he acted made me want to call it off at the last minute. Stand there and watch that bullet go through her heart, killing the human being the Messenger wants to protect. Maybe I will be able to see the way his face twists with sorrow for the first time. Maybe Vikal will cry.

Just kidding. How can I do that? I am such a good kid.

Maya is being very creative with the location where she'll take her final breath. It is the opening of a nude exhibition with hundreds of people squeezing against one another. Every man seems equally suspicious. There's a man with a hoodie covering his hair, which is as long and dark as kelp, a small man in a suit who's wearing sunglasses in a dark room, a bodybuilder who's standing in front of a painting that was obviously inspired by him. Because I knew it'd be like this, I've already planned everything in advance. I will crash the exhibition and get Maya out as soon as possible with one annoying condition: I cannot talk to her at all.

I steal a glance at the emergency alarm panel in the hall. There's a tiny red box on the wall along with a smoke detector. Everything is cloaked in a vague darkness and covered by the ornaments in the exhibition. I need to sound the alarm without anyone noticing.

I blend into the crowd. I'm wearing a yellow overall embroidered with climbing roses shaped like a bowl and a wide-brimmed hat, carrying a cute backpack with a sunflower on it, so whenever I stand next to any adult, I look like their kid. I'm trying to bottle up the excitement inside of me, since I have not been in a crowd this big in such a long time. The lights are dim and the walls are arranged like a maze filled with human breaths, the cold air from the AC units, the sweat from their skin and their chatter remind me of those nocturnal birds at the tower. I walk around, looking at all the nude portraits while trailing behind Maya. She also seems suspicious and cautious just like I do, probably aware that someone is targeting her. Even so, she still shows up in public without any bodyguards. There's a portrait that resembles Maya—a drawing of a naked woman with eyes slanted like a stray cat who's bound by tree barks and laurel leaves. Maya stops there to admire another version of herself for a bit before looking up at the crowd as if she has just spotted someone she knows. She disappears a second later.

I stand there, stranded in the centre of the maze of flesh, surrounded by all the models' sexual parts and well-shaped figures. I cannot see her from here anymore. Heart sinking, I tell myself that if Maya is this fast, she should be able to escape death by herself again this time, too. But this is actually a good chance for me to follow the plan and sound the alarm. I stride toward the red button beside a big painting in a deserted corner. I look around to make sure that nobody is there—only a glossy wooden frame behind the veil of smoke and fake clouds. However, as my finger is about to touch the red button, I am startled when I feel two eyes piercing through me. I step away from the button.

I look around to search for those eyes. Turns out that they don't belong to one of the living at all but are actually in the painting behind the smokescreen. A portrait of a person who's both male and female, lying down with their pear-shaped breasts pointing upward, their body so thin, I can see their ribs. Above their head is a halo of an ancient god. Their arrogant green eyes look down at the audience. I try to ignore those eyes and focus on the mission, but no matter where I go, those penetrating eyes follow me as if to accuse me of something. Eventually, my traitorous legs give in and go stiff. I can only stop and stare at the painting, unknowingly leaning closer and closer to it as if I am being bewitched.

'Are you interested in this piece?'

A voice greets me from behind. Turning around, I see a tall man with light-coloured eyes like a foreigner's. He has a unique aura to him and also dresses quite well. His carefree manners and friendliness make me forget Vikal's 'Don't look into the living's eyes' rule completely.

'Who's in the painting?' I ask.

This time, I broke the 'Don't talk to the living' rule. Great. He made me forget two rules in less than a minute. Even though one of my feet has already turned away from him, my body is still there, waiting for his answer.

'Hermaphroditus,' the foreigner replies smoothly. 'The son of Aphrodite and Hermes. His impressive beauty catches a tree nymph's eye, so she prays to the gods to be with him forever. The gods grant her wish by joining their bodies together, resulting in Hermaphroditus who has both male and female parts. Some call him a god, some call him a monster. It all depends on their interpretation.'

He shifts his expressive hands back into the suit pockets with his thumbs hanging out. *This man is very confident about himself*, I think. Is he the dangerous man who will kill Maya?

'How do you know so much?' I mutter.

'Well, I should know the background of my own work. A long time ago, this model was my muse. I know every inch of her body. But she refused to work with me again ever since that last time, so this is the only portrait that I have done from memory alone.'

'You sound so comfortable talking about your personal life.'

'What?'

'Nothing.'

I pretend to laugh. At least now I know that he's not Maya's lover, but the artist on display in this gallery. I take out the leaflet again. The exhibition's name is Life, yet it has been arranged in such a gloomy and dark room that the attendees don't even dare to laugh or smile. Various displays of confusion and chaos can be seen in the expressions of all the mythological Greek gods and creatures in this maze.

Once the artist sees how my eyes are fixed on the leaflet, he says, 'Make yourself at home. The Medusa, the heart of this exhibition, is in the last room.' Then, a woman in a suit walks up to him and tells him to greet a guest at the entrance. I glance at him. Other than the woman in a suit who seems to be one of the staff, there's also another woman who runs up to him with a worried face. She puts a folded piece of paper in his hand. He looks confused for a few seconds before resuming his walk.

At this point, I still can't find my target. Before I realized it, I've already walked much further away from the wall with the red button. It is quite embarrassing to think that I talked so big and told Vikal to rely on me, someone who can't control even a single thing right now. I let the stream of people push me in further, searching for Maya. Finally, after a long while, I spot Maya talking to a suspicious-looking man in a hoodie, a mysterious object in his hand. Maya suddenly strides away and out of my sight again. *Is he the killer?* My brain quickly analyses the situation. I have to choose between chasing after her or charging at the killer with only half a second to spare. My feet moving before anything else, I tackle him, aiming for him to drop whatever he's carrying. My shoulder hits his wrist hard and the item falls down from his hand and onto the carpet. I look up, despite just having fallen on my butt, and can only gape at him when I notice my grave mistake.

The object is not a gun, but a small notebook.

'Are you all right?' the hooded man asks hurriedly.

He offers me his hand, but before I can respond, a gunshot erupts in the air, shattering the lightbulbs. The hooded man is startled and quickly rushes to the scene, along with the panicking crowd. 'There's a shooting! Someone got shot!' They scream and scatter around, creating a jumble of sounds like the middle verse of the *Devil's Trill* that Vikal once played in the theatre. The sound of the second bullet pierces the room, seconds later. Then everything goes quiet. At this moment, I know immediately that it's too late to fix anything. I have to get out of here now.

8

'Humoresque'

'Damn.'

Vikal has been repeating that same word for a while now. The first time was when he saw the ghost of the artist walking absent-mindedly around the gallery at twilight with a bullet hole on his torso. Once we get back to the tower, Vikal still seems so frustrated that he repeats the word again, 'Damn,' and again, 'Damn. How did it turn out this way?' He turns to me, slouching on the padded chair, and stares as if looking for an answer. Shrugging, I swallow a grape with an audible gulp.

'Come on,' I pretend to grumble. 'I saved Maya, didn't I?'

'For that, I have to thank you.' Vikal adjusts his round glasses. The difference between outdoor and indoor temperatures fogs up his glasses. 'But are you sure that you followed every rule perfectly?'

I try to keep my laughter in check because I know he's trying his best not to let the anger show on his face. 'Of course. I swear it. One, don't stand out. Two, don't talk to the living. Three, don't look into the living's eyes. You can ask him. He was there, too. Right, mister dead person?' I elbow the artist's stomach and he is startled to see that my elbow goes through him easily. Probably not used to it yet.

The artist stares at me. I smile back, all teeth.

'Ah, yes, of course,' the artist replies, his fingers crossed behind his back, looking visibly baffled. 'Anyway, what are you guys talking about? Does it mean I'm not meant to die yet?'

Vikal sighs. He opens his book and starts reading.

'Not yet, sir. Yours is supposed to be on 9 February 20xx, which is a week from now. The cause of death is drowning at the Kata Noi Beach.'

'Woah . . . That means I've missed the chance to go to Phuket with my boyfriend before I die. Well, can you put me back into my body?'

'My deepest apologies. Your inner organs have been damaged from the bullet that was meant for Maya. Conventional medicine isn't advanced enough to save you, which might have not been the case if car users in this country made way for the ambulance. Or if the gun was pointed slightly left and the bullet hit a guest with a longer life line. Certain technical errors have resulted in . . .'

As Vikal rambles on and on, I can't help but yawn. The simple conclusion is, this artist is dead. Period. My appearance at the nude exhibition today has saved Maya, even though I didn't do anything according to the plan. But it was also the thing that kickstarted the events that led to the artist's eventual death. He died because I broke two out of three of Vikal's rules. Looking into the living's eyes and talking to the living. Interactions as small as flutters of a butterfly's wings disrupted the natural cycle of life. If the artist had not stopped to talk to me in front of the Hermaphroditus, he might have moved somewhere else where the female employee in a suit wouldn't have been able to find him. Then he wouldn't have met that unwelcome guest who shot him just because he didn't tell the man where Maya was.

'I can only send your spirit away after 9 February, so please stay here for the time being. This kid will show you around the place.'

Vikal clears his throat and spreads his hand toward me. I quickly take that as my cue to say something.

'Nice to meet you, I'm Stella, the boy you talked to at the gallery. I'm also the theatre's keeper, the babysitter, the storyteller, the furniture assembler, the owner of the bone garden, the Messenger of Death's assistant. I love books and grapes. I hate raisins.'

'A boy, huh? But all raisins were grapes once, you know?' the artist mutters while offering me his hand. 'I'm Plerng. Was a nude artist, now a full-time ghost. Also, I can't read.'

'*Plerng?* Why does a Westerner's name sound so Thai?'

'My mom's Thai. She gave me a Thai name to make it easier for everyone here. My full name is Jean-Baptiste Leblanc.'

That is how I came to call him Baptiste. It is a word related to a religious ritual that I'm perfectly familiar with. Baptism is the purification ritual for someone who would like to profess their faith in Christ. As for Jean-Baptiste, it's a French name that derives from John, the saint who led the baptism of Christ and spread God's words, according to the Bible.

Baptiste is now a temporary tenant here. I introduce him to the neighbours when Vikal is out working. The Lost Ones are excited that they finally have a new toy to play with, other than me. They hold hands in a circle around Baptiste.

'You died recently?' they ask.

'Yes,' Baptiste replies.

'Then you're the newcomer.'

'Yes.'

'Twinkle, twinkle, Little Star. Parva Stella, tell the newcomer a story.'

'Shut up.' I look up from the new book that Vikal got for me. 'I only tell you stories to make you stop crying.'

Ever since learning that he's dead, Baptiste hasn't shed a single tear. He seems to be quite happy, even. From the one minute that I got to talk to him when he was still alive, I'm assuming that he was an aloof adult who didn't like playing with kids at all.

However, the Lost Ones are super attached to him. His natural haughtiness makes the two squabbling leaders agree on granting him the leader's position.

A full night hasn't even passed yet, but they've already become close friends and come crowding into the theatre together. They volunteer to help water the bone garden and dust off the audience seats. I know that these rascals don't do it out of the goodness of their hearts but only because they think it's fun to follow their new leader's suggestions. They turn the tranquil theatre into a messy playground full of footprints and clouds of dust. Freckles swings himself from the bone rack and wrecks it. He then tries to put the pieces back together but everything is out of order. Shorty lights all the candles on the chandelier, brightening up the whole room. Two girls help each other pleat the teal curtains. Four Eyes and Fatty challenge one another to climb up the baroque marble pillars full of lichens to the round window three metres above us. I see them and can't help but sigh. What a shame to be dead and still be as graceless and clumsy as they are. They lumber up and down the pillars amid the shrieking cheerleading from below.

When Vikal returns, I am a chaotic, dishevelled mess because I've been running around chasing the kids all night to the point that I don't have the strength to even greet him. Vikal asks about Baptiste and I point to the east, outside the theatre. Seated on the window sill, the newcomer leans against the empty frame, admiring the blue hours of dawn, before he vanishes under the rays of sunlight. Vikal nods and then carries me to the padded chair in the dressing room. He covers me with a blanket and kisses my forehead before leaving to practise his violin. The requiem he always plays as a strict daily routine.

In the evening, before going out to work, he brushes my ruffled grey hair back to smoothness again.

'Can't you take me with you? It's so loud and annoying here,' I say, looking up at him.

'Not tonight.' Vikal hesitates. He already let me out once. There's no reason for me to be stuck rotting here alone anymore.

'Tomorrow?'

'Can we talk after sending Baptiste away?'

'That's a promise.'

I look into his eyes. Vikal gazes back, indifferent, then flicks his robe and flies out into the night.

9

'Traumerei'

Like every evening, the fifth and the sixth star fall onto the courtyard in front of the tower. *Thud.* Body parts splatter everywhere. The Lost Ones cheer and scream out a song while running around pools of blood and lumps of flesh. In the last light of the day, Baptiste gradually wakes up by the same window on the eleventh floor, his eyes on the brightly lit building on the opposite side of the road, undisturbed by the kids' clamour. The way he gazes longingly at the view before him, he seems painfully lonely to me. When I ask, the answer he gives me is that he used to live on the second floor of the building two blocks away. It was his studio.

'I drew everything there,' Baptiste says. 'Medusa, Hermaphroditus, Daphne, Calypso . . . My models would take turns lying or sitting down on the red sofa as instructed, among all the things scattered around the place. Maya was the one who managed the models' schedules for me because I can't read. On the building's ground floor is a cafe. The owner's galettes are coarse and quite hard to swallow but also very good. There's a creepy Goya oil painting on the wall,' he talks without looking away from the dusty window. 'I don't know what'll happen from now on. All of my paintings, the ones in the Life gallery, the furniture in the studio . . . The landlord might rent out the studio or do something else with it, I guess.'

I drag a chair beside him and sit down, chin on my hand. 'Sorry for crashing your date.'

'Hmm?'

'Actually, you were going to go on a beach trip with your boyfriend next week.' I look away. 'A week may sound meaningless for the dead, but I know it means everything for the living. I didn't tell Vikal that I broke two of his rules, but you must have already guessed that the one who made you die instead of Maya was me. If I hadn't stuck my nose into this mess, if I hadn't left the tower, you wouldn't have been shot.'

'And then would Maya have been shot instead of me?'

'There was a plan, but I messed up. Right then, if I . . .'

'It'd be better if you stopped blaming yourself, Stella.' Baptiste smiles. 'It's fine. Even if I got one more week, drowning in front of my boyfriend isn't exactly a cool thing to do.' He laughs.

I scowl. 'You think you're so cool, huh . . .'

'It's all right. It really is, Stella. It was a life well lived. I used to be quite a stubborn kid, fighting until I finally got to do what I've always loved. I got to love and make love with someone.'

'That's enough. Yuck. How can you be so straightforward?'

Baptiste laughs. Even so, his cheerfulness can't cover the ocean of regret in his heart.

According to the statistics, the Lost Ones lose interest in their new toys in about half a night, like how they have gotten bored with all the newcomers before. Yet on the second and the third night, standing in the centre of the group as the leader, is Baptiste. He's teaching them to create a gigantic piece of art from whatever the kids can find: spider webs, dead lizards, clumps of moss, and forgotten building materials collecting dust in the corners. They drag me, only watching from afar, to admire their

Sahara Desert created from toad fossils and the pink Amazon jungle made out of fortune cakes left by the electrical poles.

Baptiste doesn't stop there. He's a great storyteller as well. The man turns Greek mythology into something light and appropriate for children—using words like 'intimate' instead of 'intercourse' and 'became the stars in the sky' instead of 'died a pitiful death'. He even thinks about teaching the kids some French, justifying that the elementary school age group is the best time for kids to develop their communication skills. I tell him he's underestimating death, and that the things he's talking about only work for the living. No matter how hard he tries to teach them greetings, like *bonsoir, bonjour, enchanté,* or *comment ça va,* their memories get erased within hours. Death traps us inside the tower where the only thing that flows is the wind of the past. Not long after, Baptiste finally realizes that his effort is futile.

'It's quite strange, looking at things through the eyes of the dead.'

'How so?' I ask while munching on some grapes on Vikal's desk, arranging the sheet music that's never in its correct order.

'How should I put it . . . Ever since I was born, I'd never seen ghosts before.'

'But you saw me on the last day of your life. You greeted me yourself.'

'*You* don't count.'

He laughs. The overconfidence in his tone rubs me the wrong way, but I have to show my maturity or he will look at me the same way he looks at the Lost Ones. I don't answer, so he tries to make different conversation.

'That, too.' He points to the street outside the tower. 'I never thought that those creatures existed, some even mingling with humans. You guys must be used to them already, but I have to admit that it's quite shocking to me.'

I lean out the window, narrowing my eyes. 'What creatures? Stray dogs?'

Baptiste frowns for a moment and bursts out laughing. 'Are you kidding me?' He moves closer to me, eyes gleaming like a kid. 'There, the lumps of dust floating and wiggling on the ground. Some with legs, some without legs. Some crawl out of a human's collar. Some lumps already have the beginning of a face, climbing on the humans' arms and legs. Creepy.'

He stares at me again after he finishes.

'Huh, you really don't see them?'

'Of course, I do.' I pretend to laugh despite feeling so frustrated. Shrugging, I point at my head. 'There's one here, too, right?'

'Nope.' Baptiste's brows knit together. 'I don't see them walking around here inside the tower. Maybe there's some higher power protecting it . . . Wait, Stella, where are you going?'

Baptiste calls after me, storming off in a huff. I shouldn't have talked to him. How dare a homeless ghost like him ramble on like he knows everything, saying what is and what isn't? He can't even hear the sound of someone plastering the walls of our tower. I bite back the anger and ascend the spiral stairs, glaring down at the alleys and the tiny humans below. There's nothing except the dumpster empire of grey rats and trash.

'What are you looking for, Stella?'

Four Eyes tugs the hem of my dark green plaid skirt from behind. Startled, I raise my hand to hit him. The boy knowingly skips backward and out of my reach.

'You brat!' I screech. 'Where are all your friends?'

'I don't know,' the boy says vaguely, inexpressive eyes like clouded crystal balls staring at me. I can't tell if he's happy or sad. 'But I'll find them soon. Come with me.'

'No way.'

'Stella never plays with us.'

'And why do I have to do that?'

Now I know that Four Eyes is playing the 'giant' in a game of hide-and-seek, searching for his friends who have scattered to every corner of the tower. The game ends when the giant hunts down all the kids, no exception whatsoever. When the first light of the day touches the tower, they fall into a temporary slumber, and continue the game again once the sun sets. It is a game so gruelling that sometimes it takes them three to four days to finish.

But that's not the main reason I hate this game. When I was young, hide-and-seek was my most favourite game. My best friend and I used to pretend that Father and his students were the giants who were hunting us. If we got caught, we wouldn't be allowed to have dinner and would have to write the Bible's verses all night. My friend would always tremble with excitement and worry that the giants would find her. At the same time, she'd be afraid that they wouldn't be able to find her. There was a thin line between our pride at being so good at hiding and the sense of danger that we might go unnoticed inside the hollow of a tree until the next morning. We'd hold back our pee until the pain was unbearable. We'd be covered in sweat, crying silently until the tears ran dry. A lot of times, the game ended because she would wriggle out of our hiding place and wail, lying with a straight face that she'd gotten lost while walking back from the oratory, leaving me to be punished alone as that bad kid who'd led my friend down the wrong path.

'Anyway, what are you searching for, Stella? I can give you a hand,' Four Eyes offers while crawling under the corrugated metal sheets in search of his friends in the courtyard.

'It's nothing important.' I put one hand on my hip. 'Have you ever heard the sound of someone plastering the walls inside the tower?'

'Never,' he replies.

'What about your friends?'

'I have no idea what you're talking about, Stella.'

'And have you ever seen the weird squiggling creatures outside the tower?' The boy looks at me as if I just asked him a riddle. I quickly add that Baptiste told me a pathetic joke about those creatures that hang around the buildings and on human bodies. The more I describe them according to Baptiste, the more twisted the boy's face becomes.

'Of course. Everyone can see them, Stella.'

He gazes past the wrought iron fence, an innocent smile on his face.

'I think, one day, they'll merge and become big enough to swallow this city whole.'

10

'Poème Op. 25'

At daybreak on an ordinary day in the middle of February, I am permitted to listen to Baptiste's requiem because it is his last request.

Baptiste asked to postpone his farewell twice. The first time was when he learned that his boyfriend was still going to Phuket, according to the plan they'd made together. Ever since he became a ghost, I've never seen him that agitated. He was afraid that his lover would drown in his grief and decide to end his own life. Despite Vikal's confirmation that his boyfriend's name would not appear on the list of the deceased for a long time, Baptiste couldn't help but fret until he knew if the man had got home safely.

'Your lover returned home safe and sound without a scratch,' Vikal said the following night, his robe smelling like damask rose from a faraway garden I didn't know of. 'Are you happy now?'

Baptiste nodded. However, at the last minute, when Vikal lifted his violin, Baptiste started to panic again. He even sank to his knees and prayed to God in French, asking Vikal to stop. With my arms crossed, I watched them from afar with the Lost Ones, who constantly questioned, 'Why? Why? Why?' The scene was so pathetic that the two leader boys decided to stop calling him their big brother ever since.

'The farewell ritual should be held when everything's ready,' Vikal said, putting his violin back into the box padded with shiny crimson fabric. I knew that Vikal was lying. Every soul had someone or something they had to leave behind. Even then, Vikal still allowed Baptiste to delay the ritual for as long as he wished. I didn't understand it at all. Until the night that Baptiste had decided to be his last day, he came to see me in my dressing room and asked me to come listen to his requiem together.

'No can do,' I said. 'Vikal never allows me to listen to his music.'

'I asked him, Stella. He said yes.'

I frowned, not following. Baptiste smiled, dropping onto my padded chair without asking for permission. 'I don't wanna go through that alone. I at least want someone to be there with me. Kinda like a dog, don't you think?' he said. 'A dog whose owner takes it to the hospital for euthanasia. The owner usually doesn't wanna witness the process and asks *to wait outside the room*. They don't know that any dog would wanna be with their owner in their final moments.'

'You're rambling,' I muttered. 'I'm not your owner. If you wanna see your boyfriend for the last time, go. Stop acting cool.'

Baptiste went silent. I looked at his face and shook my head. 'Or did you already ask and Vikal didn't allow it? Oh well, Vikal can be really mean sometimes.'

'He did allow it!' Baptiste quickly cut me off. 'I'm the one who isn't brave enough to go. I'm too afraid that I won't be able to go through with the ritual and ask for it to be delayed again. That'd be so pathetic.'

After I stopped trying to convince him because I'd grown so tired of all his excuses, in the end, Baptiste gave in and went to say goodbye to his lover, five minutes before the white morning light spread and covered every part of the city. He hurried back to the farewell ritual with tears on his cheeks and sunshine in his face. I stand beside him now in my most respectable lace dress in white. Vikal is in the same ugly dark robe of his. He nods at both of us before lifting his violin up onto his shoulder. The first note screeches like a widow's cry. I watch his long, slender fingers attentively.

'What's waiting for me after death?' Baptiste whispers.

'I don't know. I haven't been there,' I whisper back.

The melody switches from fast to slow to fast again but even so, it holds all the sadness in this world. I glance at Baptiste and see that his body is starting to fade away. I realize then that I have begun to like him enough to want him to live in the tower with me forever, enough to want to kneel down and beg Vikal to stop playing. Baptiste probably notices that from my dilated pupils, so he smiles and strokes my hair slowly. I grit my teeth, trying my hardest to keep the tears from falling.

'You won't be lonely,' Baptiste says when only the upper part of his body is left. 'Ah, yes, your Vikal is really a strange Messenger.'

'Still have the heart to make a conversation?' I blurt out. 'How so?'

'His face is so expressionless, right? And the Lost Ones are terrified of him because he looks cold and unkind, aren't they? But . . . I don't know. Maybe it's just me, but I think he must have been a very gentle person when he was alive.' Baptiste laughs. The only remaining part now is his eyes. Before I can reply, the man vanishes as if he had never existed anywhere in this world before.

That morning, I lie awake in bed with my eyes wide open. Skin tingling, I flip back and forth, but it does not bring me comfort like usual. I get out of bed and the dressing room, walk to the bone garden, and nudge the little hogweeds awake to guzzle up the sunlight. The theatre is sleeping, quiet, tiny particles of dust dancing in the air. Outside the wrought iron fence, the clamour of the streets and the cars fills up the day. I've been standing in front of Vikal's room for a while before he opens the door for me. Thick curtains block all the light from entering the storage room, making it as humid as a bat's nest. I ask to be let in and Vikal scoots over to make room for me on the long sofa.

Climbing up the sofa, I bury my face in his side and cry like a dam has broken. I hit him, bitter and angry at something that isn't his fault at all. Vikal sits still, not saying anything, knowing that I am sad Baptiste isn't here anymore. He waits for the storm of my emotions to pass in silence.

'I've never seen you cry,' I say, trying to make him feel guilty.

'I'm not close to him,' Vikal answers, voice flat.

'You never hate. Never mad. Never happy.'

'That's not true.'

We are both silent for a while.

'Vikal,' I call, waiting until he responds with 'Mhmm', before telling him about what Baptiste said to me at the end. Vikal doesn't react when he hears about how Baptiste thought he was a gentle person. I ask him that if the Messenger is Death, what was he before this?

'I don't know,' he answers. 'I woke up and I'd already become the Messenger of Death named Vikal. Tons of work to do every day. I don't have time to look up things like that. I don't even know what kind of human being I was or what I did.'

'You must be lying again.'

'Humans also can't remember their past life, can they? Not even when they're inside their mother's womb or when they get their first glimpse of this world.'

'Do you know, Vikal, that humans never really forget anything?' Closing my eyes, I use my sleeve to wipe the last drop of tear off my face. 'Every memory stacks up like the piles of your sheet music. It multiplies and multiplies. A puff of wind will scatter everything all over the desk. When you want to play anything, you have to go in and dig through it all. Sometimes you find it, sometimes you don't. Without me arranging them for you, alphabetically, mind you, your life would be much harder.'

'Right.'

'Human memories are the same. We remember everything. We just don't arrange them into neat compartments. And even if we don't remember, there's someone else who remembers it for us. Even I know that I was such a weak baby. I wouldn't cry and curl up in a ball so still, everyone would think I was dead. When I got a bit older, I got pigmentation disorders and the hair on one half of my head turned chalk white. So ugly. I grew up surrounded by the villagers' pitying eyes. My mom told me this herself.'

'Don't let that bother you,' says Vikal. 'You don't have to care about the things that those people said. They're all dead. All of them.'

I smile, satisfied, and pull Vikal into a hug. Vikal trembles a little, like he wants to move away but there's no more space to do so. He cannot leave me alone. That's why he'll always remain at a disadvantage. I interlock my fingers with his. His hands are bigger than mine, the skin so pale and translucent that I can see the blue veins underneath. His fingers are bony and long like candles. His hair is down, spreading long and dark like the Nile in the illustrated book that I read when I was young.

'Say something,' I whisper. 'Play your violin, maybe?'

'I can't,' Vikal answers, his words soft and fleeting. 'It's for the farewell ritual.'

'Then,' I try to negotiate, 'explain it with words. What have you been practising?'

With difficulty, Vikal reaches around me clinging onto him, toward his desk, and hands me a sheet of paper. It's the first page of the piece called 'Death and the Maiden'. I frown, reading the notes, but the arrangement for an instrument is much harder to read than one written for a choir. The intricate symbols are confounding, so I ask him to describe the piece to me instead.

'The first thing you must understand is that this piece was originally performed by a string quartet. Quartet means there are four musical instruments. Have you heard of it before? Solo, one. Duet, two. Trio, three. Quartet, four. Quintet, five.'

'Nope.'

'Doesn't matter. Just imagine it.'

All four instruments have to play the first note at the same time. This piece needs two violins, one viola and one cello, all of them seizing the attention of the audience from the very first verse. This bright and fast tempo is called "allegro".

After that, the four instruments start to fight, the melodies layering, harmonizing and destroying one another all at once. I substitute those notes with verses from the Book of Revelation and the strange words that are vying for the thin rays of light dancing in the murky shadow behind the eyelids.

'Stay here and, please, listen to me. We must part for only a moment. You must stay here. Do you understand?'

The pleas of a girl in front of a tree hollow, on the night that the seven angels came down from heaven with a trumpet in each of their hands. The first blare came with crimson hail and rain. The second blare turned oceans to blood.

'I'll be back,' the girl said. 'I promise. You mustn't move an inch. Even if you're hungry or if your stomach hurts, you mustn't make a sound.'

Yes. I stayed in that hollow without making a single sound. Not even when the third angel blew the trumpet and all the stars in the sky fell into rivers and springs, poisoning the waters. Didn't move even when I was so scared that I wanted to run away. Even when the fourth angel blew the trumpet loud enough to strike down the sun and the moon, leaving only the eternal darkness. Deep inside my heart, I realized that the girl had left me to die inside the tree hollow. I forced a smile and cursed her, the same phrase that the flying eagle had been crying out in the sky. 'Disaster, disaster, disaster . . . will befall all the living on earth . . .'

Vikal turns slightly towards me.

'Did you say anything?'

I smile, realizing just now that Vikal's story already ended a while ago. I daydream, half-awake, half-asleep.

'No, I didn't.'

11

'Passacaglia'

The gloom from Baptiste's departure continues to mess with my dreams and memories for a while after. The visions overlap with the tune of 'Death and the Maiden' on Vikal's sheet music. The murmurs in my trance sound more and more like a doomsday prophecy. I usually dream of her in the middle of the day, when I fall asleep on the padded chair inside the dressing room. The girl with long hair in a white dress sits at my feet and reads me her book, a lilt in her voice, a smile on her lips. It makes me angry, the way her smile reflects the wavering heat of the sun. Sometimes it's not only her but also a middle-aged woman, who I think is my mom. Yes, that must be Mom because she hugs herself like there's an eternal cold that she cannot shake. Her eyes are milky and wet, a sign of insanity and paranoia, always overthinking the things people say. She sits on the back of the padded chair and sings a haunting lullaby from behind. 'Rock-a-bye baby, in the treetop. When the wind blows, the cradle will rock. When the bough breaks, the cradle will fall. Down will come baby, cradle and all . . .' Their voices harmonize like a major and a minor key, but the result is one of the most terrible tunes I've ever heard.

Dreams never let me rest peacefully. When darkness retreats and the dead leave for their bed, somebody always walks into the dressing room, then there's a murmur in my ear. If not Mom or the girl, then it's our Father. Father, who's strict with the daily prayers, Father, who lives and breathes the Holy Scripture. He stomps around the room, muttering to himself, 'Let your women keep silence in the churches: for it is not permitted unto them to speak; but they are commanded to be under obedience as also saith the law. And if they will learn anything, let them ask their husbands at home: for it is a shame for women to speak in the church.' Even though I haven't been to church for a long time now, I still remember the precise confidence of his posture. The way his hand spreads before the audience. The bright glow in his eyes. People in the community respect him because of the firm voice and the assertive demeanour that make him seem like someone who knows best. These hallucinations, combined with the city's scorching heat, can reduce anyone to madness. I flip back and forth on my back, sweat trickling down my neck and joints. The repeated tune of 'Glory Be To The Father' from the invisible piano seizes me, forcing me awake the whole afternoon. It lets me fall asleep only when night comes.

The Lost Ones storm into the theatre as soon as the sun goes down. They run up through the audience seating, screaming for my attention. When they get no response, the brats all barge backstage.

'Twinkle, twinkle, Little Star.'

'Parva Stella, tell us a story.'

'No. I'm sleeping,' I reply.

'But it's night-time,' says Four Eyes. 'Only the living sleep at night.'

'Are you sick, Stella?' asks the youngest one.

'I'm sure of it,' the leader with freckles concludes. 'It's The Living Disease.'

'Get lost. Or better yet, go to hell!' I lift my face from the pillow. There are dark bags under my eyes, my hair is all tangled and the long nightdress I'm wearing hasn't been tied properly. The kids burst out laughing when they notice my pathetic state. Hand in hand, they run around the padded chair in circles.

'If Stella has The Living Disease, we have to spook Stella. Maybe it'll cure him.'

Shorty lifts his shirt up to his neck, revealing the hole in his stomach with the large intestine hanging out like a string of sausages. The others quickly follow suit.

'Boo.'

'Boo.'

'Boo.'

'Huh, so fucking scary,' I say.

'Stella cheated. You swore,' Freckles screeches. 'I'll tell the Messenger. I'll tell him.'

That is the last straw which breaks my patience. I throw myself at the leader, biting his ear like a mad dog. The boy jumps and immediately tries to push me away, forgetting that he himself can become transparent and prevent me from even laying my hands on him. After that, I punch him in the face and all the little rats trying to stop me or get in the way. They scream more out of surprise than pain. (How can they feel any pain when they're already dead?) In the end, Four Eyes sprints up to the highest floor and calls the Gamblers down to stop the fight, escalating everything even further.

'When did you become such an aggressive kid, little Stella?' murmurs the uncle whose skeleton hangs in the toilet on the thirty-something floor.

'How dare you scold my dearest Stella? Huh, old man?' The middle-aged lady spits on the floor while hugging me close as if I were her own baby. I can hear the sound of her inner organs moving inside. 'It's because the kids came in here and disturbed dear Stella's sleep. Hey, didn't you hear me? I told you kids to leave. You can come back here and play later.'

The Lost Ones unwillingly give up and let me go. Meanwhile, I'm overjoyed that they have finally left me alone.

Maybe I really am sick because I have started to sleep at night and wake in the morning like the living. I fall asleep after Vikal goes to work, wake up and clean the theatre when he returns. Noticing this new shift, Vikal gets so worried that he dusts off the promise to take me outside at night, but now I am the one who doesn't want to go anywhere. When I refuse his offer to go outside, he merely nods, understanding, and it somehow irritates me even more. Everything he does annoys me. I throw the books he painstakingly obtained for me, crying, vandalizing the place, muttering curses under my breath. The same words that Father used with us: 'Go to hell! Go to hell!'

Vikal lets me be. Once I drop myself onto the padded chair out of exhaustion, he comes in to tidy everything up and then brush my hair.

'The Lost Ones said I had The Living Disease.' I hug a pillow, eyes filled with tears. 'Do you think so, too?'

'There's no such thing,' Vikal says.

'If I ever become one of the living, Vikal won't love me.'

'Nonsense.' His hoarse voice softens.

'Vikal, play the violin for me.'

'No.'

'Just a short one will do. Like "Hungarian Minuet".'

Vikal shakes his head wearily.

'Then go away.' I get up and push him out of the dressing room before slamming the door. 'Vikal, you dumbass,' I say, repeating the words and hugging my legs. 'Stupid, stupid.'

'The stupid one is you,' the girl in the corner of the room says. 'I told you that they'd give you no food and more verses to write if you keep acting like this.' She laughs. 'Just be nice for once, will you?'

'Shut up,' I whisper.

'Right, shut up,' Father interrupts. 'Let your women keep silence in the churches: for it is not permitted unto them to speak. And if they will learn anything, let them ask their husbands at home.'

Hearing that, the girl in the corner goes quiet while Mom, who's sitting on the back of my chair, begins singing another lullaby. 'Golden slumbers kiss your eyes, smiles await you when you rise. Sleep, pretty baby. Do not cry, and I will sing a lullaby . . .'

Standing up, I hope to escape their voices—exiting the dressing room and cutting across the audience seating. I turn around and see the girl, Mom, and Father tailing behind me. No matter how many stairs I climb and no matter how scorching the sun is at high noon, all three of them do not vanish like other spirits and the magic of the night. The prayer and the lullaby bleed into each other, the same words repeated over and over until I'm about to give up.

'What's this? You're in bad shape.'

A voice greets me. I look around but there's no one.

'Want some help?' says the voice again, rough, yet not without flair, like that of a young adult. With fingers still kneading my temple, I whisper back, 'Who's that?' It barks out a laugh and asks again, 'Want some help?'

'What's the catch?' I narrow my eyes.

'Nothing. It's out of the goodness of my heart,' says the voice. 'If you're scared of being forced into a contract, just nod.'

Seeing no other options, I grit my teeth and slowly nod. The next thing I see is the daydream that has been haunting me getting balled together and then torn to shreds like old newspapers. What follows is a loud chomping sound that disappears along with my week-long drowsy gloom.

'Nice to meet you,' the voice says cheerfully. 'And thanks for the food.'

12

'Sanctus'

'Twinkle, twinkle, Little Star . . . Parva Stella, who are you talking to?'

I quirk an eyebrow. 'Don't you hear it?'

'Hear what?'

'Don't you *see* it?'

'See what?' Shorty perks up, eyes sweeping the area. 'I see nothing but walls.'

'Poor Stella, being sick and crazy at the same time,' Freckles says, bored. 'Only crazies talk to walls.'

When I roll my sleeves up and make a fist, the Lost Ones all scream and scurry away in different directions.

Ever since being cured from The Living Disease—a temporary name for it until I find a better explanation—I have made myself a new friend. Actually, I don't think I even have the right to blame the Lost Ones for calling me crazy because from the look of it, everyone would agree with them. I cannot see this *friend*—can only hear its voice echoing through the walls of the tower, chatting with me cheerily. If I were four or five years old, Mom would explain it as an 'imaginary friend' that little kids have when they stare into empty space and talk as if there's someone there. As for Vikal, he may say that I am just 'hearing things'.

I don't want him worrying about me more than he already is, so I'm keeping this new friend of mine a secret from him.

'What's your name?'

'I have none,' it replies. 'Why don't you give me one?'

'Are you a boy or a girl?'

'A girl.'

'Even when your voice is that deep?'

'Why can't someone with a deep voice be a girl?' it asks mockingly. 'What about you?'

'A boy.'

'Even when you're wearing a skirt?'

'Why can't a boy wear a skirt?'

It laughs, loud and pleased, and then I laugh, too. The way it laughs is quite similar to that of the girl who loves to read to me in my dream. 'Who's she?' it asks.

'Why do you wanna hear about something from the past?' I ask back.

'Come on! You don't really talk to anyone here, do you?'

'I have more friends than you.'

'No, you don't. You don't talk to anyone, not even the Messenger. Otherwise, you wouldn't have been in such bad shape.'

It means the dream that's been haunting me during the day. And it's right, there's no one I can call a friend in this tower.

'Her name is Fatima,' I say. 'One of Father's eleven Little Lambs. She used to be my best friend.'

'What's a Little Lamb?'

'Little Lambs were the eleven girls who were responsible for important tasks in the church,' I say. 'The girls were six years old and above, wore white lace dresses, and didn't have to do labour work. When they talked, the Little Lambs' words were beautiful and melodious as a song, since they had all grown up in the choir room. Inside the chapel, they would sit in the front row, helping

Father with the rituals, and they would even sit with him at the dining table, listening to stories from the outside world that only Father knew, since he was the only one with a telephone in his bedroom. They grew up with desserts, fruits, fresh milk, fish, and good-quality meats, while the boys, who were responsible for the general drudgery, got only a share of the previous day's bread and a pie with scraps of meat on the bone as a filling.'

'Even religious institutions are hierarchical,' the voice observes. 'You were one of the Little Lambs, too, weren't you, Stella?'

'Of course,' I say, tossing a grape into my mouth. 'I'm too adorable not to have been.'

'Why eleven, though? Can't there be more Little Lambs?'

'Nope.' I shake my head. Our Father was very particular about the number of people at the dining table. The path to the dining room was decorated with stained glass that depicted *The Last Supper*. Jesus, surrounded by his twelve disciples, arguing about the mysterious traitor among them. 'The number thirteen is a bad omen,' I explain. Including Father, the number of people at the dining table couldn't be more than twelve. Whenever any of the Little Lambs got their first bleeding, they would be cast out and made a normal citizen. And then Father would accept a new Little Lamb from the village.

'A normal citizen?' the voice questions. 'How many people were there in the church?'

'There were the eleven Little Lambs, Father, disciples and maids. Around twenty people in total,' I recount. 'There were about 300 people in the village. We all knew each other. We were a small agricultural community living up on the mountain. We could even see the sea from there. The disciples would drive a pickup truck out of the village to buy stuff from the nearby city once a week. On Sunday, everyone would gather at the church. After the service, they would line up for their share of supplies.

Some nights, the teenagers would come to the church and borrow the video player to watch movies. The movies that Father allowed them to watch.'

The voice listens to me and lets out a soft 'Huh' that echoes the walls. I ask if something is wrong.

'How many years ago was this?'

'Mmm, around three years ago, maybe? I didn't keep count.'

'Three years?' it wonders.

'What about it?'

'Nothing, nothing. Just not what I expected.' It laughs. 'I thought that was during ancient times, but it was only three years ago. A place like that still exists in this day and age, huh?'

'What do you mean?'

'Nothing. So, what do you think about the outside world after you got out?'

'Nothing,' I repeat its own word, annoyed.

It laughs.

The voice reminds me of the Lost Ones in that it loves nagging me to tell it stories. But the things that it wants to hear are not bedtime stories. It wants the past. Every time I give in and reveal the little things in my past, it asks about how I feel. A lot of times I realize that it says that to ruffle me. One time, I expose its plan, thinking the accusation will stop it from continuing. To my surprise, it easily admits to its intention without a pause.

'I can't help it. Your negative thoughts sustain me.' It giggles thoughtlessly. 'Those who died at a young age don't understand suffering. That Messenger is dangerous. If I just went and ate his emotions without permission, he'd kill me. The old people upstairs are tasteless, their tastes as pathetic as their deaths. And it takes ages for that plastering man to come here. That's why I'm relying on you.'

'You know the plastering man, too?!'

'Of course,' it answers. 'That's my creator.'

'He's . . .'

I bite my tongue, but it's too late. It knows now that I covet that information, so it won't reveal the rest. 'Name me,' it offers. I imagine it as a human being sitting on the opposite side, smiling like the cat that got the cream, the trump card in its hand. 'Babel,' I try.

It goes quiet for a while before replying, 'Not bad'.

During the time that Babel and I talk in secret, Vikal starts to get more serious about taking me outside the tower for some fresh air. He blames himself that I got sick because he has been leaving me alone in here for too long. I don't say anything, since I'm the one benefitting from his decision and since it's a promise he made a long time ago—on the day we first met.

Poor child . . . You've seen enough of the world's vice. You deserve a rest.

If you come with me, you'll see more of it. Is that what you want?

The image of him in the robe with padded shoulders, his hand stretching out to me, those long, slender fingers he used to play the violin to send spirits to the underworld. I have been expecting to walk alongside him as an assistant ever since that night, but his answer has always been 'Not yet'.

'Are you done?'

A low, hoarse voice cuts through the dim glow of the candles in the dressing room, pulling me back to the present. 'No,' I call back.

'What's the problem?'

'The dress is too short.'

'I just bought it a few months ago. It shouldn't be.' Vikal crosses his arms and watches me turning this way and that in front of the tall mirror. 'The sun's setting,' he rushes me. 'Don't forget your shoes.'

'The shoes you brought me last time, they don't fit me anymore,' I complain. 'Wrong size, maybe?'

'How's that possible?' Vikal clears his throat and walks into the room. He goes down on one knee and opens the box containing a pair of light pink ballet shoes before trying to put them on for me. 'They really are too small.' He gives up after a while. 'It's a shame. These are genuine lambskin leather.'

I stretch the leg with the shoe still dangling from my toes.

'Hey, Vikal.'

'Mhmm?'

'Can spirits outgrow clothes?'

Vikal doesn't answer. I can hear giggles from the walls.

13

'From the New World'

'The deceased is Mister Mongkol, thirty-two, the groom-to-be. He died from a heavy blow to the back of his neck. No weapon found around the area, no signs of resistance. The crime scene is in the parking lot of X hotel. The surveillance cameras have malfunctioned, so we need some time to recover the footage. The deceased's belongings are not missing, which indicates that it may not be robbery homicide.'

'Have you checked his phone?'

'I have, sir. No data of any calls made in the past three days. The logs and messages have been deleted, along with the texts on his social media accounts. There are no fingerprints on the phone. The culprit must have wiped them off after erasing all the data that could be linked to them.'

'Other than the bride, did anyone else drop by the hotel to meet him?'

'His family—father, mother, younger brother . . .'

'Cops are so cool.' I'm sitting on a chair, enjoying my vanilla ice cream and red jelly. The image and voices of two police officers are projected from Vikal's thick round glasses that he's set on the table so we can watch together. We're inside a bar that looks like a small English church from the outside. Other than the three people at our table, there are also two bartenders alternating between shaking out drinks and rereading the remaining orders. Weirdly dressed drinkers are seated around the corners of the bar. A pale man sits at the counter, muttering something unintelligible to himself, looking absolutely despondent. No one in this bar acknowledges the presence of the strangers seated a few metres away—as if they've been ordered to stare blankly into their glass and drown in their own memories while Dvořák's Symphony No. 9 is blasting from the gramophone in the background.

'Tomorrow's my wedding day.'

Mister Mongkol, thirty-two, is staring at us.

'I loved Wipa. I've always been devoted to her. I even paid for her family's massive debt. But last night, that guy suddenly showed up. That son of a bitch is her ex. I was stupid to go there without telling my family. I didn't want Wipa to see him. Who could have known that they've been in it together? Wipa is the only one who knows the passcode for my phone. Bastards!'

'Huh . . . What kind of careless plan is this? What would the woman get for helping her ex kill her husband-to-be and then getting caught?' I hear the bartender's voice cut in.

'She's not that bright,' says the bartender's assistant.

'The culprit is Mister Prasert, thirty, the bride's secret lover. He's an ice sculptor at X hotel.' Vikal flips open his book of the dead and jots down more details with a blank expression.

I raise my hand. 'The weapon was ice, wasn't it?'

'Correct. It already melted down the drain with all the rain in the evening,' says Vikal.

'He managed to carry the ice all the way to the parking lot without being caught on camera. That's pretty good. There's no blood splatter, either. Look, by the time the police figure out the cause of death, the culprit would have already destroyed the evidence and disappeared. No one knows if the lost footage can be recovered. Mister Mongkol here was pretty careless to go to such a secluded place alone.'

'However, the fact that the camera couldn't pinpoint anyone should already lead to the conclusion that the culprit was possibly someone from the hotel. And, to an extent, the phone's passcode can actually tie the bride to the crime,' the bartender adds.

'We'll leave the rest for the forensic and the IT staff to figure out. We've already done enough,' says Vikal.

'Wait.' Mister Mongkol raises his hand. 'You told me to tell you everything so I did, but what now?'

Vikal puts his glasses back on, fingers interlaced on the table. I turn back to the ice cream in front of me, eating it while staring at the blocks of ice slowly melting away inside the groom-to-be's whiskey glass.

'Your data has been recorded. Thank you for your cooperation,' says Vikal. 'Next is the farewell ritual.' Bending down to pick up his violin case, he places it on the table and opens the latches. Vikal turns to the bartender and asks, his head tipped politely, 'Please let me use your place tonight, master.' The bartender chuckles, telling him that he has no problem with that, and has also been missing the sound of Vikal's violin anyway. The man then gently lifts the needle up from the record player while Vikal braces the violin on his shoulder, his middle and ring fingers pressing on the fingerboard. The whole bar goes quiet as if everyone is holding their breath, but as Vikal sets the bow on the strings for the first note, a loud screech erupts from Mister Mongkol.

'No! No! Not like this!'

Vikal stops, his eyes behind the glasses narrowing slightly. He knows what is about to happen.

'You guys aren't here to give me justice?! Go get that murderer's soul! You reap what you sow, isn't that right? Or is the world so fucked up that even a fucking reaper doesn't give a shit about blatant injustice? Why did a good man like me have to die while that killer walks free?' Mister Mongkol spits and throws the whiskey glass at Vikal. It hits his forehead and drops onto the floor, broken into pieces. 'If you don't have what it takes then give me your power! I won't leave! I'll stay here until I get my revenge . . .'

The Messenger listens to the demands of the spirit who doesn't seem to be able to calm down. He doesn't respond or try to justify it, not even saying that he doesn't have the power to interfere with a human's death, like he kept telling me before. Vikal seems so cool and kind and it is starting to upset me. No one should dare raise their voice at Death, and especially not Vikal. He is my caretaker. He is mine. I am the only one who can raise my voice at him. Who the hell does he think he is?

'Don't be so full of yourself.'

I enunciate each word with the depth I only use when I scold the Lost Ones, but Vikal raises his index finger in front of me, a sign for me to stop. Mister Mongkol, who paused because he was surprised by my outburst, resumes his tirade of profanity. This time, he settles on a long story of the love and devotion he had for Wipa. He goes on until the curses and contempt turn into moans and misery, tears flowing from his eyes. He drops his head onto the table and sobs when the finality of his death kicks in at last.

Vikal offers him another glass of hard liquor and the guy finishes it in one go. Vikal opens the small pouch attached to his belt and takes out the pocket-sized scriptures of various religions in case the man wants some help calming down. He refuses, before sitting down with hands clasped together to show that he is ready.

'Can you help me?' Vikal whispers to me.

I turn away from him. 'No can do. He threw a glass at you.'

'It didn't hurt,' he confirms. 'You've sung this title once. The same rhythm as the one from the gramophone earlier. Can you do it, my assistant?'

I pout. Vikal prepares to play again without waiting for my answer. I sigh and stomp forward to stand at Mister Mongkol's side. When I touch his palms with my fingers, he suddenly grabs them, his grip tight like a baby's. I can feel that he is trembling like Baptiste when he was trying to act tough. I bite my lip. The thought of Baptiste brings the storm back into my heart. The violin plays the first note—largo, slow, unhurried. I close my eyes and automatically sing the soprano part of the song.

'Going home, going home, I am going home . . .'

I sing. The spirit next to me is crying.

'Quiet-like, slip away—I'll be going home . . .'

It's only normal. Everyone cries when they realize that they are dead—that's what I tell myself. Vikal's notes are leisurely and relaxed, soothing and gentle. His eyes are fixed on the other's soul, until the man gradually fades away, peaceful like a sleeping baby inside its mother's womb. Once the song is over, the customers in the bar give us a round of applause. No one acts like the farewell ritual is something odd.

It was my first farewell. I sit there, leaning on Vikal's shoulder wearily, my chest heavy like when I was drowning in grief after Baptiste's departure. *Is this the weight of duty?* I think while sipping my cola. This is what Vikal has to face every night after the sunset. Record the cause of death, listen to the dead's curses without responding. I really wonder if the other Messengers are also like this. If I were one, the night wouldn't have ended so well once someone threw a glass at me like that.

'The Messenger's work is more complicated than I thought,' I murmur.

Vikal glances at me, waiting for a clarification.

'You feel sorry for every single one of them. You want to help them get justice. But the only thing you can do is play them a song and bid them farewell. So, you think the things you do are useless. You feel bad so you just stand there and accept all the curses thrown at you, since it's the only thing you can do for them. This job is depressing.'

Vikal does not answer. He looks up and closes his eyes, exhausted.

'This is why you practise your violin all the time, isn't it?' I touch his long fingers. 'You don't want me to be sad. That's why you didn't let me come with you before . . .'

Vikal squeezes my hand softly as an answer. He then murmurs, soft like a feather.

'Someday, you'll have to face sorrow,' he says. 'Loss, goodbye. I only wanted to stall and keep you safe from all the dangers for as long as possible. I want you to enjoy your childhood for a little longer. But then we can never escape sorrow, can we?'

I laugh. 'Grapes that grow into raisins are sad, too, aren't they?'

'Not all grapes become raisins. Have you never thought about a good thing like wine?'

'Do you think I have more chances to grow into wine?' I joke.

Vikal opens his mouth to say something, but at that moment, the bartender walks up to us and says that the bar is about to close. Vikal quickly picks up the tab and pulls me up from my chair. We're going back to the tower.

Baptiste was right.

Vikal really is gentle.

14

'Habanera'

Once I understand the burden of the Messenger's work, I make up my mind that I will stop acting like such an insolent child and teasing poor Vikal. I have stopped asking him to find me all the lovely things I like—accessories, clothes, and the piles of books huge enough that it would take me multiple lifetimes to finish everything. Vikal is surprised that I don't dirty my clothes anymore. And I have stopped talking back and acting out all the time. I can even boast that starting from the sunset following my first farewell, I have decided to fully devote myself to the duty of the Messenger's assistant. I cut off the sleeves of the old dress that doesn't fit me anymore and sew it into a bag for the thick leather tome Vikal uses to store the final records of the dead, the sheet music folder, and those tiny pocket-sized scriptures that Vikal often carries around on his belt. I beg him to let me carry everything for him, so he doesn't have to wear that ugly speckled robe again. I spend three days trying to convince him that the ridiculous robe makes him look more like a fat and bulky black cuckoo than the graceful Messenger that he intends to be. Moreover, when he walks, the crackling synthetic leather rubs against itself, making pieces of the ancient material rain down on the floor like confetti.

'Lately, you've been going out of the tower every day, Stella.'

Babel greets me from the wall, its booming voice echoing in the dressing room, shaking the leaves of the potted plants. I woke up a little while ago and am in the process of stuffing myself into a dress with a ruff. It used to fit me perfectly, but now I can barely wear it without tearing the fabric. When I stand up, I notice that my limbs are starting to grow long and wiry like tree branches, looking uglier than I can stand. 'The Lost Ones have been saying that they miss you, their kind and beautiful babysitter who tells them stories,' my invisible friend keeps flattering me. Its sweet talk begins to resemble what Fatima did to Father, more and more. 'It can't be helped.' I zip myself up with a struggle before turning to talk to it. 'This babysitter is incredibly popular and is super busy every night. He doesn't have time for those worthless rascals.'

'How's the outside? Is it fun?'

'Come with me if you wanna know.'

I've been trying to get Babel to go outside with me, but its voice has never been heard beyond the wrought iron fence even once. It simply tells me that the time for that hasn't come yet. It's just scared of Vikal—that's what I think at such times. How could I ever know that its real reason is the complicated conditions that need to be fulfilled, or that it has something to do with me in the future?

Left, right, left, right. We walk past streets full of cars. Vikal keeps repeating that we cannot look into the living's eyes and that we cannot talk to them, not even a single word, because whatever we do affects the others' fate. Left, right, left, right. We make a turn at the corner of the building with allamanda bushes and into a small alley, past the old lady sitting in dirty rainwater on her mat with a deck of cards. Nocturnal birds crowd on the transformer, chittering about the depressing deaths caused by the plague and how their workload increases because of it. 'Be careful not to walk under them,' says Vikal. 'Real or fake birds, they still poop on people's heads.' I laugh while hanging onto his arm and giving them a wide berth. Once we're already past the area illuminated by a gigantic fake moon hanging above a bookshop that looks like it's going out of business soon, we arrive at an alley with a cute name: Ghostwalk Alley.

All shops here at Ghostwalk Alley are only open for the people who live after the sun sets. It's a special area bathed in lights so dim that it becomes difficult to distinguish the dead from the living. Rows of fluorescent street lights flicker on and off like a scene from a horror novel.

'Do the living come this far in?' I ask.

Vikal thinks for a moment and says, 'The bartender from last night is also human.'

'Unbelievable.'

'But the assistant isn't. And the customers aren't really.'

'What's the assistant? And what are the customers?'

'The assistant is an official like me,' he says, and then quickly adds, 'Not one of the Messengers. He's in another department, and a high-ranking one at that. I can't tell you the details. The customers are varied: ghosts, demons, people from the past, from the present, from the future.'

Left, right, left, right. Bars, bookstores, tailor's shops, food markets. I enjoy the area every time I visit. As I'm munching on a chocolate-filled wafer in front of the kind witch's candy house, Vikal waves at a barn owl perched on the roof of the library. The owl flies down before transforming into a beautiful woman, and then asks us for a cigarette. Of course, we don't have one. Vikal introduces her as an independent Messenger, not working through any agency. Her duty is to send the souls of those not on the list away, like the ones who die before or after their designated time, the vengeful spirits, or the ones taking their own life. 'Most of the time, they don't let me send them away, dear child,' the barn owl complains while blowing plumes of smoke. 'When they see me, they run like dogs with tails between their legs. They're so attached to their old life that they'd rather be stuck in the same place than move on. I can only help those who are ready and call for me.'

'Why are people who commit suicide so attached to their old life? Sounds quite contradictory, doesn't it?' I ask.

'That's right. Has Vikal told you that one story, child?' The barn owl pinches my cheek lovingly. Seeing Vikal shake his head, she continues without waiting to see if anyone wants to listen. 'More than a hundred years ago, Vikal had the name of this one man in his list of the dead. But years earlier, the man committed suicide. He was a servant who chose to end his life with poison following his master's death. The man asked to be put in the same coffin as his master so that the servant could follow and serve him in the next life as well.'

'How romantic.' I use my sleeve to wipe the crumbs off my face.

'Oh, no, my child. They didn't get to meet in the next life. The master was gone for good, but the spirit of someone who commits suicide will go through that miserable moment over and over again. People who jump off the building will keep on jumping. People who drink poison will linger around their painful funeral procession every day. Until one day, something shifts in their soul. Their heart goes numb, little by little. The last time I saw him, he didn't even remember why he took his life or who he did it for. He's turned into a demon.'

'That's unfair,' I argue. 'He died by his own will.'

'It's not about anyone's will. This is the system.'

She puts out her cigarette in an ashtray above a trash can.

While the mouth of the alley is full of entertainment, located in the deeper part of Ghostwalk Alley is a branch of the Messenger office. Once in a while, Vikal visits the Department of Records to submit the logs of the spirits that he's sent away and walk out with the list of names for the next month. I ask him how trustworthy the Messengers' logs are and how much of that is true when everything in there comes from the spirits whose judgement might be clouded by anger and resentment, like Mister Mongkol. Vikal explains that the department already has all the information, and that the logs from the Messengers are only to verify if everything checks out. The registrar, who has been listening to our conversation, interrupts, saying that they simply want the Messengers to confirm the status of the spirits who have departed, and that other Messengers don't actually record every single detail like Vikal. I then ask him why he has to be so serious about it.

'Because the dead are not just some data in the system.' Vikal clears his throat, his deep voice trembling slightly. 'Everyone used to be alive. Everyone was human, once. We must record the story from their point of view, too. No matter how biased or vengeful they all sound, I accept them. When they're gone, at least there's one person who still remembers.'

'Do you remember all the spirits you've sent away?' I ask.

Vikal nods. Right then, I don't really understand what he means. However, after three months of working as his assistant, I discover that apart from helping me accurately note down each and every detail of the dead, record-keeping also imprints the presence of those spirits in my memory: appearances, voices, overflowing tears, scents of their souls, clothes that they wear, people they love and had to part from, people they hate, and the belated realization that the things they'd been fighting for their whole life are a waste of time. I tell Babel everything once I get back to the theatre. I shake off my shoes, pull off my stockings, and take off the thick velvet dress before draping it on the back of the padded chair. I hug my naked legs and complain non-stop. Babel listens to everything I say and asks the same old question: 'How do you feel? How do you feel?'

'That lady died because a bullet fell from the sky. Can you believe it?'

'Can a bullet fall from the sky?' the invisible friend asks.

'Someone in town went mad and fired a shot into the sky. The bullet fell onto her head while she was going back home from work. She didn't even realize what was happening. Poor thing.'

'How do you feel about this, Stella?'

I think about it. 'I pity her, maybe? Why?'

'Nothing. But I think you've grown a bit. Before, you never cared about anyone or what would happen to them. You were heartless, like the kids.'

'I'm still like that, though,' I mutter.

Babel laughs. As I'm about to fall asleep, a hand as cold as the dead's brushes against my hair and gently pets my head. Startled by the touch, I wake up with a scream on my lips.

'How can you touch me?!'

'Ah, haven't I told you?'

It sounds delighted. With eyes wide open, I see two white arms growing out of nothing. Two hands and ten fingers move freely and reach for me again while the centre—where a torso, legs, and a head should be—still looks like a squiggly ball of dust and hair inside a trash can. I'm shaking like a leaf—it's a scene straight out of a nightmare. What Baptiste said before is coming back to me.

'It's quite strange, looking at things through the eyes of the dead.'

Babel's right arm drapes across the part that is supposed to be its chest, bowing a little.

'I've grown, too.'

15

‘Dance of the Goblins’

‘Stella, do you know what “whale fall” is?’

Babel says this while stroking my head with its cold, damp hand.

‘Whales that die in the middle of the sea are huge. For a while, their corpses float on the water; a grand feast for scavengers like sharks. After the sharks tear all the fat away, the carcass sinks to the deeper parts of the sea, becoming food for smaller creatures. Thousands of metres more and the currents drag it down to the seafloor, and now the creatures of the deep like worms, shrimps, or even deep-sea sharks, come in and gorge on it,’ it tells me.

‘There are worms in the deep sea?’ I ask.

‘A lot of them. Sea worms are even more disgusting than earthworms. After the small critters finish off the carcass, the big critters come and devour them. The skeleton under the deep sea, where the sunlight can’t reach, turns into a complete ecosystem in itself. What do you think? Isn’t it interesting?’

I look up at it, still not used to the strangeness of its form that consists of only two white arms and a twisting ball of dust. It combs through my pale white hair while continuing with the story. ‘This tower is like a whale fall. It’s a fall of civilization, a discarded and deserted ruin that turns into a swamp full of ghosts, suicides, and pitiful children.' Its voice doesn't contain even a drop of sympathy.

Babel was born out of the corpse of an eight-year-old girl—the first one who died at the hands of a depraved man in his thirties. That man was obsessed with slight frames, big round eyes, and children's innocence—like all the other serial killers out there. He learned to hide his perverse urges behind a smile. On the outside, he was a kind elementary school teacher who always carried snacks and toys around with him.

'He never touched his students. No, Stella, he wasn't that stupid. His targets were the children who got separated from their parents in deserted alleys. I don't know the details of how he found each of his victims. The first time I became aware of my existence was when the girl's hopeless scream echoed off the walls for the last time.'

'What?' I spring up. 'Those kids said that they were stabbed to death before being stuffed inside a sack and dumped here.'

'Are you sure they said that?' Babel laughs. 'Are you sure that they truly understand their own death? The most unreliable thing is human memory, especially little kids'. Look at you, for example. How did you die, Stella?'

'Our church got burned. Everyone died. I died in a tree hollow.'

'Do you really believe so?' it asks.

'No, wait, there was a survivor. That girl, she left me to die in the hollow and ran away!'

'Do you really believe so?' it asks again. 'What about the cause of the fire? What about the other villagers? The Little Lambs? Your Father and his disciples?'

I close my eyes, trying to find my way through the shadowy maze of my mind, but, in the end, nothing resurfaces. The events from that time have been completely erased from my memory, and even Father's and Fatima's faces look like oil portraits that a stranger wielding a palette knife scraped into a messy ruin, in contrast to the glimmering images of my youth that still play out as vividly as the day they happened.

'I don't know, Babel.' I sigh.

'It's not your fault. Memories are always deceptive. The more people talk about them, the more unreliable they become, just like how the Messengers' logs of the dead's last memory are actually useless to the Department of Records,' Babel says cheerily. 'I'm saying that it's true that the kids were stabbed and then put in a sack, but they weren't dead yet. That man didn't want to stab anyone to death. He only did it to stop the victim from moving. He always beat the sack from the outside when the kid tried to struggle, and eventually the kid only laid there motionless out of fear, whimpering pitifully like a small animal that got shot by a hunter. That really turned the man on.'

'That's enough. Disgusting.' I cover my ears.

'You really don't wanna listen? I'm telling you what you wanna know the most,' it says, voice high and pretentious, both hands shaking my shoulders excitedly. 'He made little holes in the tower's walls every day while the crime was still being planned, until there was enough space to store the sacks. When the time came, he mixed wet concrete and plastered the hole closed with red bricks while the kid was still alive. He even left a small hole in the sack, so that the kid could still breathe, and then died a slow death in the wall. And then he would put his ears against the wall and happily listen to their final cries. And in that moment, I was born, the man and the Lost Ones, my creators.

'The second kid, the third, the fourth, and the police still couldn't catch him. The fifth, the sixth, the seventh, the eighth, their parents searched for them, hopeless and scared. My beloved Stella, you have no idea how much I long to meet him again. I've been hiding his traces from the Gamblers and the Messenger, but I don't even have to try with the Lost Ones. Every time he appears, sated after he plasters the wall, the kids that have been growing in number will run to their favourite babysitter in front of the theatre. They refuse to understand the things that happened to them and distract themselves by demanding more stories, forcing you to be Wendy, a kind, loving mother to the Lost Ones, while they fight for the role of Peter Pan. What's more, they run away from the Messenger who tries to send them away, because deep down, they know in their hearts that they won't be able to have peace if their pitiful parents can't find their bodies. And I'll keep growing if no one does anything about it.'

I widen my eyes.

'What about tonight? You've grown again . . .'

Babel doesn't answer.

I struggle under the weight of the hands on my shoulders, heavy and unmoving like a pair of iron pliers, forcing myself to stare into the wriggly ball of dust where the face and the eyes should be, and seeing only empty darkness staring back. I think it is beaming. I try my best to shake it off, snarling and biting like a wild dog. It lets me fall to the floor. I grab my robe and quickly put it on before running out of the dressing room.

'It's too late,' the invisible voice mocks from the walls, the creeping vines trembling. 'Last night, he came and left while you were enjoying the world after sunset with the Messenger.'

'Shut up,' I scream. 'Where are the kids' bodies?!'

Babel laughs, pretending not to hear me. I open the theatre doors. Bright light immediately pours in, piercing my vision. Morning is here. The dead return to slumber. The air is full of pollution and the living's chatter from the road. I inspect the tower's top floors one by one, desperate, feeling for any traces of the children. The twentieth floor, the thirtieth floor, the fortieth floor, I still cannot find a place that can hide a body. The fortieth floor, the thirtieth floor, the twentieth floor, I walk around in circles until exhaustion overcomes me, dragging my legs and pulling my eyes closed. I wake up again when the Lost Ones surround me at dusk.

'Stella's awake!' the leader with freckles announces. Four Eyes and Shorty high-five each other cheerfully, spluttering that they have been searching for me. Luckily, a Gambler auntie saw me collapsing on the stairs while she was doing the shooting star parade from the top floor.

They are still as jolly and enthusiastic as ever. Even though they were brutally murdered, even though the number of the victims have been increasing, they never have to worry about a single thing, heartless creatures like them. I grab the skirt of the girl with the Little Mermaid print. 'You guys . . .' I whisper, struggling to get the words out. 'Do you remember, where your bodies are?'

She stares back at me with her crystal ball eyes.

'Parva Stella, what are you talking about?' the little girl asks.

'Poor Stella. You must still be sick,' says Lanky. 'You're sick, you're mad, and now look at you, you're becoming an adult.'

'An adult?!' they cry out, alarmed. 'We hate adults.'

'Shut up . . .' I whisper, my voice dry. 'Please, I'm doing this for you.'

'Twinkle, twinkle, Little Star. Parva Stella, you've been gone a long time. Tell us a story,' the second leader interrupts. 'Look, our newbie won't stop crying.'

I look at the new girl, sobbing in the middle. Her face is wet with tears, her eyes red and swollen. But that's all right. Soon they will turn into murky crystal balls, empty like everyone else's. I bite my lip, feeling so small for not being able to do anything except telling them stupid stories that will keep them from waking up from their eternal dreams. That evening, I try again and again to ask them about the locations of their bodies, but to no avail. When Vikal calls me to accompany him to work, everything returns to how it once was every night.

16

'Ode to Joy'

The violin plays the farewell tune, the air void of the singing that usually accompanies it. The latest farewell goes on without a hitch, the dead fully cooperating and willingly adding their story to the Messenger's logs. When it's near closing time, Vikal puts the drinks on the running tab for the officials. I place the violin and all the tools back inside the velvet case. The world of night always becomes sleepy and sedate after midnight. Tonight, the bartender leans over the counter to look at us and asks why I stopped singing halfway through.

I don't answer. Vikal tells him that I don't feel well tonight.

We walk out of the bar together, my shoulders drooping all the way back. I hang my head, trying to stop the tears that have been brimming ever since the moment that my attempt at the usual soprano came out sounding like a goose's grating cries. Shocked, I covered my mouth and escaped to the side, amid the curious stares of the customers in the bar. Vikal seems to understand the reason, so he doesn't try to initiate a conversation. Once we reach the fork between the dressing room and the musical instrument storage, I grab the hem of his shirt.

'Will you find a new partner if I can't sing anymore?'

My voice is so hoarse I almost cannot recognize myself.

Vikal turns to look at me, bemused. 'No,' he replies. 'I'd been working on my own for a long time. I'll just go back to that.'

I can tell that he didn't say that to please me. The answer makes me feel relieved but, at the same time, it is blunt and cruel, since it's almost like he's saying that I never mattered much to his job in the first place. I slam the door shut behind me and drop onto the padded chair, crying. Vikal knocks softly on the door and then leaves when he doesn't receive any response.

From the darkness, Babel reaches out with its white arm that seems slightly longer than before and strokes my hair slowly.

'You didn't do anything wrong,' it says. 'You're just hitting puberty.'

Its fingers fondle my neck, poking at the tiny Adam's apple lovingly.

'Go away.' I slap its hand away. 'I don't wanna see you anymore.'

'Sure,' it replies, indifferent.

I never *see* it again after that. However, its manifestation becomes even more terrifying. Babel comes back as sounds, sounds that indicate that it's still following me around everywhere. The sound of claws scratching walls, like a woman's screech, echoes in the tower. The sound of gigantic feet dragging across the floor and knocking over all the bone racks in the garden. The sounds tell me that Babel is growing again, even though it has been a while since the last body was buried in the wall.

The Lost Ones begin to notice its existence, too. Four Eyes asks about the inexplicable cracks on the walls. Fatty says he saw long arms and legs in a white dress running around corners and goading them to run after it. The youngest girl says that whenever she plays tag or duck-duck-goose, there is always an extra person in the group, and once they count again, that extra kid is gone. As for me, the dream-like gloom has returned, filling the daytime dressing room with Father's gibberish prayers and Mom's haunting lullabies. One day, the pain in my head becomes too unbearable, and in my delirious state, I pray for Babel to come back and eat my nightmares again. As if answering my prayers, in an instant, it rushes back to tear the apparitions apart and devour them, finishing with a loud belch. It is at that moment that I see its current state of existence. It's been growing rapidly, no longer the friendly invisible voice that I knew.

It's turned into Fatima. Fatima with unnaturally long limbs, over two metres tall from feet to neck, dressed in the white dress from my memory that was swallowed. The unfinished head is still a swirl of dust with strands of hair poking out, facial organs rolling everywhere. The eyeballs are where the mouth should be, mouth instead of ear, ear instead of nose. It turns to look at me, beaming.

At that moment, only one word flashes into my mind: Titan.

Fear and disgust win over my ego. Swallowing my pride, I visit Vikal's room and ask to sleep on his narrow bed again. He welcomes me without a question and doesn't even scold me for abandoning my assistant duty for weeks, because he assumes that my emotional instability is his fault. Poor Vikal. I don't deserve to be close to a good person like him. I use this opportunity to press myself against him, laying as close as I can, closing my eyes and savouring the cold scent of death from his long dark hair, flowing on the bed like the Nile. His lovely and stunning features, the wrinkles on his clothes, his long violinist fingers—all of these things put my mind at ease. At the same time, they stir a nameless fire inside me. Before my thoughts wander into an even wilder territory, I whisper with my new voice, hoarse and ugly, in his ears, 'Even if I do bad things, you won't leave me, right?' Vikal widens his eyes slightly, confused. Poor Vikal. He's the only one who doesn't know about the things happening under his nose. No surprises, really. If those evil swirls can hide the murderer's traces from everyone in the tower, hiding from the Messenger isn't too complicated to achieve.

Especially with the Messenger's assistant as an accomplice . . .

'If I confess to my sins, you cannot be mad at me, okay?' I say.

Vikal frowns. 'It's strange that I'm hearing this from someone who's been trying to rile me up.'

'That's because I really did mess up this time.'

I take Vikal to the dressing room where Babel is waiting. It is clear now that it has taken over this room. Babel is admiring its hideous figure in front of the mirror. My beautiful clothes are scattered across the floor. With its bulk, it only has to turn left and then right to knock over everything in the room. Babel is too absorbed in its own reflection to notice us. I'm surprised that it doesn't even try to hide from Vikal.

What if it doesn't have to hide from Vikal anymore?

The thought sends a shiver down my spine.

Vikal is still as calm as ever. He goes back to the storage for his violin and asks me to look for a certain farewell piece in his piles of sheet music, explaining that this thing is a demon, born from the worst of humans' negative emotions. It can be found everywhere with ghosts, and sometimes clinging to humans' bodies. It's completely normal. 'It'll only get stronger when it has a name,' he says as he sets the violin on his shoulder.

I'm too ashamed to tell Vikal that *that* exactly is the worst thing that I have done. I have given it a name.

I let Vikal place the bow on the violin's strings, playing the holy tune and murmuring a cleansing spell that only nocturnal birds and demons understand. In that moment, Babel begins to realize that its existence is being threatened. It whips toward us and shrieks a high-pitched cry, shaking the theatre's floor like an earthquake. Babel rages and pulls the chandelier that has been hanging firmly from the ceiling for decades past, down to its swift end, tearing the teal curtains off the hook and letting in the bright light of the living world. The sun reflects off the crystal beads scattered across the floor, livening up the audience seats that are covered with moss and lichen. Vikal keeps trying to do what he's been taught, not understanding why his cleansing spell is not working. I quickly drag him away from the demon's hand before he gets crushed against the wall. Grabbing all the necessities within my reach, I pull him into a run, escaping along the stairs under the clouds of dust. Vikal's movement is slow in his human form, so I tell him to turn into a cuckoo and fly away without worrying about me. 'Meet me at Ghostwalk Alley tonight,' I say. Vikal reluctantly accepts. I watch the black cuckoo flying away into the sunlight, and then stumble away myself, fear in my throat, along the path of the living.

Yes, we have to leave our beloved tower, just like that.

17

'Gnossienne no. 1'

In front of Ghostwalk Alley, the barn owl is the first one to spot me standing there, clumsy and awkward, with a precarious armful of objects: Vikal's violin case, a bag full of sheet music, a pocket watch, and ribbons. She tilts her head by ninety degrees, like a typical barn owl, scrutinizing my unkempt appearance. Hair dishevelled, clothes torn and dirty, knees grazed and bloodied, feet bare and covered with scratches I earned from running down eleven floors of the tower and then along the roughened sidewalks to get to the destination. 'You must have been through a lot, dear child.' She strokes my hair, her touch soft and light. A dam breaks and a cry escapes me, hoarse and unfamiliar. I let her hold my hand and lead me to the nearby cigarette shop to tend to my wounds. 'Your voice has cracked. That's so cool. You're a grown-up now,' she consoles me while offering me a cigarette. 'Here, the taste of adulthood. Try it.' I shake my head, explaining that Vikal will definitely get mad if I try. The barn owl giggles and praises me for being such a good kid.

After the wounds are treated and I receive a new pair of shoes, we take a walk along the alley to wait for Vikal. The barn owl buys me a steaming hot ham and egg sandwich for me to stop being sad, because she doesn't know how to deal with sad people. I munch on the sandwich, the warmth and the salty grease spread from the tip of my tongue down to my chest, making me smile. The barn owl asks if I have ever noticed that the shops in Ghostwalk Alley are never the same for every one of my visits. The people of twilight are fun-loving people and they tend to move the shops around as they please. One day, this alley may even be moved to another corner of the city. She even tells me that once in a while, she gets into a violin duel with other Messengers in an inn for some extra cash. 'Independent Messengers don't get any fringe benefits. The authority doesn't allow us to put our food or drinks on their tab like the officials, so we have to save up from submitting the logs of the souls that no one wants to deal with,' she says. 'The violin duel makes good money. The audience is the judge, and even if I lose, I always get some tips from them.'

'Why don't you wanna be one of the officials?' I ask.

'I want to be able to choose.' The barn owl places a cigarette between her lips. 'I do this because I want to talk to the dead. Plus, it's fun, doesn't make me sad like you and Vikal.'

Tonight, Vikal's favourite bar is closed. The English church exterior has disappeared like it had never been there before and has been replaced with a stall of an old ex-Messenger selling ugly, fetid robes. I remember the robe hanging at the front. It has the same navy pattern as Vikal's fat cuckoo robe; every single one of them has huge, padded shoulders. A photo of a respectable-looking Messenger hangs next to them. That must be the image that tricked Vikal into buying it. The thought pulls a sudden laugh out of me in front of the stall owner. When I tell the barn owl, she bursts into laughter, a loud shriek of delight, before instantly flying away once the old man raises his cane at her for startling him.

Half the night passes before Vikal finds us. The barn owl and I are inside the bookshop with a gigantic artificial moon floating above its roof. Even though the owner has decorated the interior with only a few lamps, the shop is still full of people sitting in corners, reading for free. As I'm deciding between Chekhov's

The Crooked Mirror and Jackson's *The Lottery*, Vikal's stormy face appears between the gap in the books on the second hand shelves. Startled, I back into the stacks of damaged books waiting to be fixed, knocking everything over. A weary sigh can be heard from the owner, who is sharpening a knife using his leather belt on the other side.

'I've been looking for you since sundown,' Vikal admonishes me.

The frustration in his eyes and the frown on his brow endear him to me so much that I leap forward and pull him into a tight hug, scared that he would disappear again. When I look up at his face, I notice the vanishing gap between our heights. Before, Vikal seemed incredibly tall and huge, thanks to that cuckoo robe. Now my head already comes up to around his shoulders. This is the first time that I am thrilled about my unwelcome growth.

'I said,' Vikal pushes my shoulders away and clears his throat, 'I've been looking for you since sundown. Where have you been? Why didn't you wait for me in front of the alley?'

I shake my head, offering an apology. Vikal turns to the barn owl, who pretends to cover her mouth as she giggles. We realize instantly that she's been messing with us. 'I like to see you lose your cool, once in a while,' she says. I think she only wants to irritate Vikal—like me—but even so, Vikal is more relieved than mad. He thanks her for patching me up and then explains the whole situation to her.

The barn owl takes us to the Messenger inn, located on a narrow path that branches away from Ghostwalk Alley. This place looks like a building that has been repurposed for swiftlets' nest farming—smelling of sewage, exploded with feathers, the din of the nocturnal birds' chatter blanketing the space. 'Only freelancers stay here. Bear with it.' By 'freelancers', she means independent Messengers, herself included. I understand the meaning of her 'bear with it' a little while after, when the freelancers start to practise their violins simultaneously, each of them playing a different tune. Vikal and I have to cover our ears and shout at each other inside a room with paper-thin walls. Music and whispers continue until dawn. That is when we get to rest, under the light of the living world.

On the first few nights, I feel agitated about losing the theatre on the eleventh floor. However, it doesn't take me long to get used to the commotion of Ghostwalk Alley, the constant ruckus of my neighbours not allowing me enough time by myself to cry and think about my beloved boneyard. Once the sun sets, I follow Vikal out for work, which he still religiously does every night. We didn't carry all the beautiful dresses from the tower's wardrobe with us, so Vikal has to borrow some clothes from the other Messengers, women and men with slight frames, who are willing to help out a kid like me. Since I have not worn anything besides dresses for a really long time, the plain-coloured shirts with no patterns that ordinary people wear make me feel bare and naked, while pants make me feel awkward about my long legs that only seem to get longer and longer. 'Not cute at all,' I mumble to my reflection in the mirror. This insecurity blinds me to the fact that, in this dimly lit Ghostwalk Alley, no one cares about my appearance as much as I do.

My current assistant duty remains only to help Vikal carry his violin case and a bag of sheet music. When Vikal plays a farewell melody, I step aside and hum a tune with my goose-like voice that I want no one to hear. Later, the barn owl tells me that I am a tenor, the highest voice for men. 'Of course, it's lower than the soprano voice that you sang in when you were younger, but it's not a goose voice. There's nothing to be ashamed about.' She says that I will get used to it and be able to make use of it, one day. Vikal never pressures me to sing when he sees that I'm not ready, and even gives me my share of the payment from log submission, allowing me to buy snacks in the alley as I please, even though I haven't been doing much for him these days.

After work, I spend the rest of the night reading books at the bookshop for free. The owner recognizes me when I tell him that Vikal bought the books here for me when we were still living in the theatre on the eleventh floor. He remembers every single book he's mended, along with its new owner—as if the books were his children. Similar to other shops in Ghostwalk Alley that keep moving around without a pattern, his bizarre bookshop opens only on the nights that his lover has to take care of some business abroad and he feels lonely with nothing to do. This means that on nights without the bookshop, I have to relocate to somewhere else, such as the inn's common room, where string musicians from everywhere gather and show off their skills. Listening to violinists and cellists with fierce strokes, I am immersed in the wild waves of sound until morning, after which I drag myself back to Vikal in our room, my heart still pounding, like a pot of boiling broth.

Vikal has no time to enjoy that kind of entertainment. Once he finishes his work, he comes back to the room and pens a report about the new demon that can be a threat to the living and the Messengers, for the authority. He flies back to the tower in his cuckoo form to spy on it. Vikal keeps his distance, careful not to be noticed by the Gamblers on the upper floors and the Lost Ones on the lower floors. 'Your children are fine. They're still playing hide-and-seek inside the tower. And the Gamblers are still doing their parade at nightfall. There's no need to worry,' he says while softly brushing my hair. 'Nothing changes in the world of the dead who are stuck in the past. No one cares that the babysitter and the Messenger who used to live there disappeared.'

I know that he says that to comfort me. I know that he wants me to forget the time I spent in the tower, so that he can keep me out of the danger that he's about to completely involve himself in. But it's already become impossible for me not to be a part of it, and to begin with, I am the one who kickstarted the twisted disaster in the tower. So, when Vikal, who sounds like he hasn't had a single good night's sleep in a long while, mutters, 'If we knew the name of the demon, everything would be a lot easier,' there's no chance of me ever stopping the words from spilling.

'Babel.' My eyes meet his. 'Its name is Babel. I named it myself.'

18

'Spiegel im Spiegel'

Vikal's reaction is tamer than I thought.

'Is that so?'

Then, only silence—leaving me apprehensive that I'd be reproached or banished from the room. I quickly apologize, just in case he's still deciding whether or not to be angry with me, but then he shakes his head and says, 'No, it's my fault'. How is it his fault when the one who talked to the demon, fell for its trickery, and gave it a name, is me? 'My duty is to protect you, but I was negligent enough to let you face everything on your own. My duty is to introduce you to the details of the world after sunset, and yet I kept the things you needed to know a secret.' He massages his brow and adds, 'All because of one stupid reason.'

'What reason?'

Vikal doesn't answer.

A short while after he submitted a report about Babel, the authority responds by sending over a Senior Messenger to directly take care of the matter. The news about this arrival silences the nocturnal birds at the inn that are normally quite rowdy and prompts them to clean up the tables and form neat lines on both sides of the door, as if they were welcoming someone with an invisible red carpet. Excited to see a bigwig from the Messengers' community, my jaw drops when I notice that the person who appears on the imaginary red carpet is an old lady with cataracts and frizzy hair, her gait unsteady, despite the help of her cane. Afraid she would collapse, I can't help but approach the woman and offer her a hand. The old lady whips her head toward me and beams.

'The allamanda boy!' She greets me. 'I remember you. The good kid who gave me water.'

Vikal walks up to her and bows respectfully. He introduces her as the bat hawk, and me as his assistant. The bat hawk listens and frowns, shoving her crooked nose into my face. 'Ah, I know. I see it now,' she intones with the voice of a fortune teller. 'The Moon, The Queen of Swords, The Tower . . . Yes, yes, it's almost time. We have to hurry, Vikal!'

'Yes, ma'am.' Vikal stands at attention, awaiting her order.

'To cleanse a demon of that level, we need four Messengers.' The bat hawk's tone gets more serious as soon as she talks to her subordinate. 'String Quartet, one cello, one viola and two violins. I'll bring the fish owl with me. You have to choose someone with whom you can play well. A freelancer's fine, too. Now, give me a name.'

Vikal glances at me, who has never laid a finger on a single musical instrument in my life, before turning back to name the barn owl. The bat hawk stretches, cracking her back, saying she is a good choice, and then tells the onlookers to call the barn owl here; they're going to hold a meeting. They dedicate one room of the inn for the occasion and put up a sign that says, 'AUTHORIZED PERSONNEL ONLY'. I protest when I'm not included in this meeting, since I'm the one who knows about Babel and the conditions behind its growth the best.

'We've learned enough from you, dear boy,' the bat hawk replies without turning back. 'A demon that's been given a name is deadly, but we've faced its type before. We'll just focus on the farewell piece.'

'I'm Vikal's assistant. We work together,' I insist. 'I may be able to lure Babel out, it reacts to me. Trust me, I'm useful.'

'You're only afraid that you'll be left behind, my child.' The bat hawk stares into my thoughts with her blind, merciless eyes. 'And I'm afraid we must do that.'

All four of them disappear into the meeting room all night. The melody that slips through the gap under the door is merely the sound of their rehearsal, an attempt to play in tune with one another. The freelancers flock to the wall, trying to eavesdrop on the Senior Messenger's cello mastery, but because of their avian nature, there are only the sounds of *krrr woo krrr woo–chirp chirp–woooo woo woo* of the nocturnal birds who are bickering for an optimal spot or pooping on each other's heads. I give up and return to my room in the end. Once dawn breaks, I poke my head out after hearing the meeting room's door slam open. A young man saunters out, hunchbacked and lips turned down into an arrogant scowl, supposedly the fish owl. '*Hoot*, *hoot*, *hoot*, *hoot*, don't you have anything else to do, you dipshits?' he screams at the crowd and spits. The freelancers hop away in disgust. I watch them from afar until the storm abates and then finally spot Vikal walking back to the room.

Vikal seems dead on his feet. He ignores me and goes straight to his bed like never before, which I find exceptionally odd. I put a damp towel on his forehead, hoping it will ease his exhaustion somehow, but instead Vikal takes the cloth away and stares at me with the kind of intensity that makes my cheeks warm. At that moment, I notice the swollen red bruises under his eyes as if he has been crying. Assuming that he must have been reprimanded by his superior officer, I pull him into a tight embrace.

'What did that old hag do to you?' I mutter, gritting my teeth. 'What did she say?!'

'Wait, what are you talking about?' Vikal seems confused. 'You have misunderstood.'

The situation is strange. No matter how much I ask, Vikal doesn't explain the cause of his swollen eyes and keeps on glancing at me up and down, an inscrutable longing in his face. It feels good at first, but his stare makes me more and more nervous, so I spring up and walk out for some fresh air. Vikal mumbles like he doesn't want me to leave, but my legs are already taking me away from the room. They lead me to the only friend who will tell me the truth behind Vikal's tears.

White light shrouds the city as well as the stone tiles littered with the feathers and spittle of the night birds. I knock on the wooden door to the room under the stairs. A long and languid 'Mmmmm' can be heard from inside before the barn owl drags herself to the door, her lovely eyes leaden with sleep. I have to talk to myself for a long while before she finally wakes up and responds. I ask her why Vikal cried during the meeting.

'Ah.' The barn owl exhales heavily, her nostrils widening. 'You're here because of that.'

Since she's not working for anyone, the barn owl readily discloses the secrets of the authority to me. 'I don't care how powerful that Senior Messenger is. I only accepted this mission because Vikal said my name and I think it'll be fun. All right, first things first.' She rocks her shoulders and withdraws her legs under her body in a bird-like manner. 'This is about the demon in the tower. And you.'

According to the reports and evidence that the bat hawk has gathered, Babel is categorized as a demon which dwells in a building. It can conceal itself within the structure of a place, and no one can detect it. The ultimate solution is to destroy the building. Once there's nowhere to possess, the demon will lose all its power.

'In this case, we can't do that because the forty-seven-storey building is too big. That's where the second method comes in.'

This kind of demon is a ball of negative energy that accumulates. It grows when it receives food, which is an enormous amount of negative feelings or memories—like the fear a person feels moments before being killed.

'If four Messengers show up at the same time, that demon will definitely go into hiding. Therefore, we have to take advantage of the split second when it opens its mouth to eat and becomes temporarily defenceless. That's when we'll cleanse its spirit with our melody.'

'Wait.' I raise my hand. 'When it opens its mouth to eat. You mean . . .'

The barn owl places a cigarette between her lips, her smile fading.

'Do you know the fish owl? The guy sucks at viola,' she says. 'Vikal's senior called him here because he happens to have this one kid on his farewell list.'

The barn owl puts a document on the desk: 'Pafhun, 7, 13 December 20XX at the deserted forty-seven-storey tower.'

Short, but enough to make me feel nauseated.

'This kid is the next victim in the serial killer case,' the barn owl says the words that I don't want to hear the most.

'Vikal cried because of this?' I ask. 'He knows that I can help him change this girl's fate. He only has to ask. I've done it before.'

'It's not that.' The barn owl scoffs, the sound is kind and sad at the same time. 'A Messenger's tears don't fall merely because a stranger is going to die. But it's because someone he loves will give away his life to alter destiny.' She then places another document on top of the girl's photo and looks up at me.

The person in the new photo is me. A boy with a shock of messy white hair, a beautiful puffy dress. The photo says that he will die on 13 December 20XX at the deserted forty-seven-storey tower. Exactly the same thing as the girl's.

'My dear boy, you've already set your mind on stopping the murderer since the beginning. It's not about Vikal at all. You just can't stand it if someone else gets killed at the tower again.' The barn owl blows a white plume of smoke into the air. 'Vikal asked me to stop you.'

'I don't understand—'

'The reason he doesn't stop you himself? You know him.'

'No.' My lips are shaking so much that I almost forget how to speak. 'I don't understand . . . I've been dead for a long time.' I stare at the Messenger, silently begging her to laugh and say 'Of course. Not a funny joke, is it?' But the barn owl doesn't do what I want her to, not even turning away from me, like Vikal likes to do. She stares back at me, motionless, listening to my silly words. 'I'm dead. Three years ago, in the tree hollow. Our church was burned down. Father, the Little Lambs, the disciples, nobody survived. No, my close friend, she ran away and left me there alone. She . . .'

That girl . . .

What was her name again?

Fatima?

No.

'I've warned him that it's useless to take care of a human child,' the barn owl says. 'Listen to me, you're not dead. You have never been dead. Has it not been clear enough? You've been growing every day. Your voice cracks. You grow taller. Your hair gets longer. Your old dresses don't fit you anymore. You bleed when you fall.'

'No. It's not true. I'm already dead. In the village on the hill, three years ago . . .' I argue without believing a word I say. As tears start to fall, I eventually give up, a lump of grief blocking my throat and stopping me from saying anything else. My tears flow like the crystal beads from the chandelier in the theatre on the eleventh floor when it dropped onto my beloved boneyard, destroying everything. The barn owl sits there, watching me shatter, pity in her eyes. Vikal lied to me. Everyone lied to me. No, *I* lied to myself. My mind wanders back to the evening when we stood there together, our gaze lingering on the orange sky, watching the nocturnal birds fly in an upturned V formation. '*Sometimes they appear before it's time. As an omen.*'

'What for? Mental preparation?' I had asked him then. Vikal had shaken his head and said that it was because sometimes the Messengers were biased, just like humans. Those words take me back to the first time I met the Messenger who pulled me out of the tree hollow. A male cuckoo clad in black with a strange navy pattern that was designed to enlarge the wearer's shoulders. I was crying for the end of the world. Next to me was a girl.

I remember her name now.

Her name was Stella.

19

'La Campanella'

Stella was the name of an eleven-year-old girl in a white lace dress who always sat in the front row at the morning worship. On her lap was a songbook with a pristine red cover. She turned it to page forty-three where the song 'I Surrender All' was, singing with her angelic soprano voice without ever having to glance at the lyrics. Everybody knew that the other Little Lambs were envious of her voice, which was like a gift from God. Her skin was clear and pale like a china doll, her eyes round like a doe, her lips red like a fully ripe fruit. Her manners were impeccable, indicating that she had been born in a wealthy and strict family, the modest yet vibrant character that she had toward everyone attracting the eyes of the adults, who both admired her and felt bad about their own ageing body because of it. She was brought there by the disciples when she was three years old and died with everyone else on the day the world ended. But that is a story for later.

Next to her on the same bench was Fatima—a kid of the same age who was the only Little Lamb in this place who was never jealous of her best friend. Despite Stella's beauty and the privileges that adults fought to offer her, both children saw through each other's façade at first sight, and shared the hobby of laughing at the villagers' blind, stupid devotion to Father.

Before Fatima could be named, a nameless baby was born on the darkest ill-fated day on the unorthodox calendar. His birth was two months early, triggered by his mother's grief at being abandoned by her husband and condemned as the wife of the greedy disciple who had stolen Father's silver and disappeared without a trace. The day the baby boy was born, there were only the mother and a midwife in the room, both worried sick about the baby who wouldn't open his mouth and cry, no matter how much they hit his bottom. The baby was barely breathing.

'He won't survive. Even if he does, he won't have a long life,' the midwife said, exhausted.

Hearing the finality in her voice, the mother didn't know what else to do except wail as if her heart had been ripped out of her chest. Tears falling on the baby's face, she prayed and begged that if her son survived, she would give him into the hands of the Holy Spirit, and he would serve Him and attend to religious duties for the rest of his life. After the words left her mouth, the baby started to bawl like a dying swan, his soprano voice loud enough to quake the earth. Seized with immeasurable happiness, the mother fell unconscious. In her sleep, the mother mumbled 'the Lord's mercy is endless' over and over, scared that the baby would suddenly stop breathing.

After the first time, the baby cried every chance he got, thanks to the sickness that typically came with a premature birth. Not trusting anything in this world, the baby cried and asked for his mother all the time, but for an unknown reason, refused to drink his mother's milk. The child grew up sick and small, often catching a high fever and losing his appetite, and was severely underweight. His hair turned white from the lack of melanin, and his development was slower than other kids his age. Fatima didn't speak until the age of three, and the first words that came out of his mouth were 'disaster, disaster,' which immensely frightened his mother and led her to wrap the child in fabric and pray for His mercy for three days and three nights. That incident stopped the boy from speaking again for another six months. In the first three years, the mother never took Fatima out to see anyone, the first reason being that she was embarrassed about the sin her husband had left her with, and the second reason being that the boy's hair was matted like a mucky rag. She couldn't bear the thought of her child having to endure the condemnation of the vicious villagers, so she chose to work hard and raise the boy inside her home until the story of the traitorous husband and Fatima's existence faded from everyone's memory. Even the midwife, who died four years later of dengue fever, did not remember that she'd ever delivered the baby who wouldn't cry.

The boy often played with his tiny penis when he didn't have anything else to do. The mother chastized him for such behaviour and stopped him from ever doing that again ever since he was a little over two years old. Her shouts could be heard three houses away as if the existence of the penis was an evil thing that would bring about the family's ruin. She taught him to ignore his own sex and raised Fatima like one would a lady. She taught him table manners, such as sitting up straight or using the various spoons and forks, and also inculcated in him the habit of keeping silent in front of strangers. When the boy turned five, she sacrificed her only pink tablecloth and tailored it into a pleated dress for the boy to wear to the church for his grand opening.

She did not do this only because she held a grudge against her ex-husband. In a small town with a population of only 300 people, everyone's duty had already been decided. The children went to study at the church. Once they grew up, they would have to work hard. Men would work in agriculture and any construction work, which required physical strength. Women would kill the cattle for food and clothes. When her son, who was her whole world, was born sickly and weak, the last thing that Fatima's mother wanted to do was to send him away to do hard labour. She then turned to the last resort—the church under the rule of a pastor who called himself 'Father'.

Father, the only leader of this town, was an exceptionally wise middle-aged man. He inherited a confident demeanour and an alluring voice, as a great cult leader should possess from the last Father, whom he had been in no way related to by blood. His vague childhood memories seemed to have been erased either by some kind of medicine or some other brainwashing techniques of the last Father. Years later, he also used the same technique with the scores of babies who were brought to the church by questionable means. One of the babies was the young lady Stella, who was destined to marry the son of a billionaire in the future if her parents hadn't looked away from the baby's stroller at a department store that afternoon. The girl was dreaming about a garden with talking flowers when she was grabbed and taken into a van, along with another group of children, and eventually ended up as the adopted daughter of a villager who couldn't bear a child of their own. With Father's gift for brainwashing, it didn't take long for the kids to stop crying and force themselves to forget their real family, their survival instinct compelling them to strive and pull through without a choice. Every child in this peaceful agricultural town was baptized, and, in exchange, the sparks in their eyes were lost forever.

Other than his exemplary ability to rule, the other thing that couldn't go unmentioned when discussing Father was his eleven Little Lambs. Girls, aged six to twelve, would trail after him in a line, a songbook in each of their right hands, and speak only when they were spoken to, led the church in prayer or sang. The rest of the time, they would be still and silent as statues, head bowed in modesty, in their intricate embroidered dresses.

It was not easy to become one of the Little Lambs. Father never showed up to teach anyone in class, but would select the girls from the annual worship ceremony or on any normal Sunday, when a Little Lamb retired. Fatima's mother had thoroughly studied his unique tastes. She had done everything she could to mould her baby boy into a beautiful lady that Father would love; taught him how to curtsy and sing prettily, exactly how Father would like. Even though it had taken both of them a lot of effort to get there—she'd had to hit him with a belt, since Fatima had been vocally protesting against the future that she'd set out for him—the boy had eventually bowed his head in defeat and agreed to do what his mother had wanted him to.

'If you become a Lamb, my life will be easier, too. Do you understand, my love? Even if you retire when you're twelve, you can always continue as a disciple. Teaching is way easier than toiling. You'll thank me later. Get it?' She kissed his face over and over until the boy's face became wet.

Fatima didn't get it, but whatever.

Fatima was already used to how his mother pushed him around as she pleased. What thrilled him more were the eyes of the villagers in the church that stared at him when he first appeared at a candlelight service. 'Who's that kid?' they whispered. 'Cute,' they said, 'Yes, very cute.' No one had ever said that Fatima was cute before. Because of how sickly he'd been, his mother had caged him in the house, so he'd never realized the extent of the beauty that'd been bestowed on him before. Small hands that had never carried a heavy object. Pale smooth skin that had never been touched by sunlight. When he bowed in front of Father, he could sense that he was being scrutinized as if he was prey to a drooling hound. Fatima knew right away that he would be selected. What he didn't realize was that Father, whom everyone loved, was merely a disgusting brute in the guise of a respectable pastor.

20

'Orpheus and Eurydice'

For a child who had never experienced human selfishness and cruelty, in Fatima's eyes, Father was simply an eccentric middle-aged man. A man who preached about humility and hardship while he cut the best part of the meat for his eleven Little Lambs in order of the love he had for them. Young lady Stella sat on Father's right, the seat of an archangel, pouring him red wine and making sure that the silver goblet in Father's hand would always remain full. The other Little Lambs ate their food in a ladylike manner, never raising their heads, never making a sound. Fatima sat at the end of the table, pushing grapes around on his plate with a fork, and hoped that Father didn't have anything else to teach them so that dinner would end soon and he would be able to go run around in the field.

For the first half of the year, Fatima's mother was worried that the truth about her son's gender would be exposed. Hallucinations that she and her son would be excommunicated from God's sacred land haunted her dreams and waking hours. She couldn't eat or sleep, and even planned to sneak into the Little Lambs' living quarters with a giant knife to cut off her son's penis. Fortunately, the disciples caught the middle-aged woman wandering in front of the church with a knife and took her back to the weaving mill. From then on, she was listed as a crazy lady and banned from the church grounds forever. This trivial news never reached Fatima, who spent his entire days practising his singing and studying the Bible.

The truth was, other than his best friend, Stella, Fatima planned on keeping the lie about his own sex a secret until the end of the world. Since he had been a baby, he was taught that having a penis was a sin and that it'd alienate him from the others. He would never go into the shower if the other Little Lambs or disciples were there. He wouldn't let anyone touch him and would bite anyone who tried to take his clothes off. Even Father got his hand slapped away once in front of everyone when he tried to pull Fatima up for a kiss on the cheek during the storytelling hour of the Little Lambs.

'Good girl, don't you love Father?'

Father's voice was like ice on Fatima's skin. The boy played along, saying 'I do', and then glanced at him with disdain like he was a parasite. Father stopped short and, from then on, started to see Fatima as a stubborn child. His irritation eventually turned into apathy. Fatima's importance among the Little Lambs continued to dwindle, to the point that Father stopped sending anyone for him if he was missing from the dining table or the Bible class, letting the lost Lamb run and eat on his own.

The loyal disciples thought that Father was already tired of the boy, but they didn't realize that even though the other Little Lambs had been changed many times in one year, Fatima was still sitting there at the far end of the table. The person whose eyes were sharp enough to see it was the six-year-old sitting at the head of the table, young lady Stella.

One late afternoon after class, Stella sauntered up to the boy, who was playing by himself under a gigantic rain tree a great distance away from the church.

'I'll share my toys with you if you teach me how to climb a tree.'

The girl was smiling when Fatima looked up. He didn't care about the toys, but was curious about why the number one Lamb, who was supposed to be snuggling up on Father's lap, would want anything to do with him. Still, it made Fatima quite proud of himself, so he taught her how to climb the rain tree. 'Hang on to this branch and step on the stub,' Fatima said while swiftly jumping from branch to branch. The girl did as instructed, missed the step on her first try, and fell on her butt. Her cries were loud enough to be heard by a disciple, who was walking past the area. He dropped the buckets of water he'd been carrying and ran toward the children immediately.

'Who did this?'

Father's voice was calm, his fingers intertwined. Stella sobbed and pointed at Fatima. His punishment was to sweep the rain gutter and have no dinner that evening. Fatima was surprised when the cheeky little lady secretly climbed up to his balcony with half a loaf of bread and sour Christ's thorn jujube jam. He shook his head, still mad at her. 'You two-faced bitch. This is why nobody likes you,' Fatima insulted her with the words he'd heard from his mother. Stella flushed, her ears beet red. She had never had anyone saying that they didn't like her before, but still kept the promise she'd made—sharing her toys with Fatima. A wind-up tin rabbit with a drum; a snow globe with a penguin flapping its wings in front of an igloo, snowflakes swirling around when shaken; and books. Fatima had never seen any book other than the Bible before. He didn't understand the content alongside the illustrations in Stella's book at all, but it pushed him to become the most attentive student in the Bible class.

Stella never sided with Fatima in front of Father. She betrayed him and always let him get punished alone for the things they'd gotten up to together. But despite that and everything else, their friendship bloomed and the two children grew unexpectedly close. Fatima could see through the girl's tricks. Stella agreed to do the things she didn't like in exchange for the things she wanted. When the disciples were allowed to drive into town to buy more supplies, she would receive books, newspapers, or photographs from the outside world, which were forbidden in this sacred land. Fatima repaid her by revealing that he had a penis and letting the girl see it. They ended up keeping each other's secret without having to promise anything.

Stella didn't give up on climbing trees. Fatima taught her to start from the smallest mango tree before moving on to the purging cassia with thicker branches, until she finally conquered the rain tree. Both children gazed at the distant sea from the top branches, the church small and insignificant below them. Fatima turned to look at his friend, hoping for a victorious cry, but instead, the girl's face was full of tears.

'I miss home,' Stella said. 'I miss mom.'

That was when Fatima learned that the girl was the only one of the kidnapping victims who had never forgotten her real family. She'd had excellent survival instincts since birth. When asked if she remembered any past events, she'd lied with a smile and acted so docile that no one had thought that she would need more medicine, while the other children kept on bawling without pause. When Fatima used his stubbornness to get away from the adults' perverted hands, Stella had already surpassed him with the idea that she was going to run away from here.

'Suppose one of you has a hundred sheep and loses one of them. Doesn't he leave the ninety-nine in the open country and go after the lost sheep until he finds it?'

The eleven-year-old Stella read the Bible to the boy, before saying that it was something Father liked to refer to when the disciples asked what he would do to a stubborn Little Lamb like Fatima. 'Father's obsessed with you,' the girl added, not concealing the hatred in her voice anymore. 'The poor wrinkly old man. You only have to pretend to love him, and then maybe someday we would be able to tag along with his disciples on a trip into the city. Someone out there will be able to recognize me.'

Fatima didn't know what to say. He knew that his best friend was trying to convince him to join her top secret mission, but he was incapable of pretending to be something he wasn't. Even his unstable mother could only teach him some basic manners like a proper curtsy and a good posture. Just thinking about having to fawn on Father like Stella made him want to vomit.

Stella called him stupid for not even trying to do something this simple. She turned away from him and towards the other girls. That night, she disappeared from the bed near the window. Fatima went out to look for her and found the girl crying inside the hollow of the rain tree.

He hugged her. Warm tears flowing onto his pyjamas.

'I miss my mom,' Stella wept. 'This is a prison. This is a nightmare. Sacred land nonsense. This whole town is insane.'

Fatima didn't really understand the feeling of someone who'd had to part from their family. He only wanted the girl's wish to be fulfilled.

'If I get out of here, I want to go to the sea,' he told her.

'Will you think I'm stupid, if,' Stella sobbed, 'if I think . . . mermaids are real?'

'Of course, they are,' he replied.

They fell asleep inside the hollow, dreaming about a colourful world outside and a vast sea. Fatima kept repeating to himself in his dream, afraid that he would forget everything when he woke up, that from now on, he would do whatever the girl asked him to, no matter how much it pained him.

But the chance never came.

The thing that came, not by anyone's wish, was the apocalypse.

Everything began in the twelfth rainy season of their lives.

21

'Danse Macabre'

The citizens in Father's Holy Land hadn't heard anything about the outside world for over thirty years. It could also be said that three-fourths of the population had already forgotten how this mysterious town had been founded. This went all the way back to the time before the first Father had turned into the founder of the cult.

The first Father was a speaker who travelled from one place of worship to another across the country. His speeches always included the idea of the land of purity, which earned a lot of faith and donations from believers who longed for a sufficiency economy in this capitalistic world. The money eventually turned into a town upon a hill in the west. Father selected a number of believers to build an agricultural settlement with a church being the centre of power. Time passed, and one day, the first Father realized that the outside world was being invaded by modern technologies, so he built barbed wire fences and appointed guards to protect this town of virtue. His citizens learned to survive on the blind love and faith that had been passed down from generation to generation.

However, not long after, Father's agricultural project was halted due to a population issue. Every year, the elders died and the young believers weren't able to produce enough children to sustain the town. The absence of modern medicine resulted in a number of deaths that could have been avoided if antibiotics had been available. Babies died during natural childbirth. The lack of clean water for daily consumption and the spread of diseases in contaminated swamps . . . The first Father was not a coward who would give in to easy solutions like modern medicine and public utilities, so he had his disciples go out and bring back healthy babies to raise on Father's Holy Land. One of the children was the current Father, the successor of the late Father's rank and spirit, both.

During the twelfth rainy season of Fatima's and Stella's lives, the current Father had to face the issue that the first Father had been afraid of.

The coming of the 'outsiders'.

A bronze van with a sticker saying 'Journalist' stuck on it was parked just outside the barbed wire fence. The head of the group was a bearded muscular man who introduced himself to the guard as 'Jeab' and explained that he worked with a documentary channel on YouTube. He wanted to do a story on the agricultural project that had gone viral on the Internet among netizens who had too much time on their hands and accidentally found a hidden town on Google Street View.

Of course, these terms sounded too unorthodox for the guard to understand. He couldn't make a decision on his own, so he contacted Father. When Father refused, he ordered them to leave immediately. However, the journalists from the outside weren't as docile as the followers whom Father could push around any way he wanted. Jeab and his crew brought out their tents and camped right in front of the fence, refusing to leave. When the disciples left the town on Saturday to buy more supplies, Jeab tailed them in his van and even interviewed the locals whom they'd bought the goods from.

Father now understood that he was dealing with dogs with a bone, so he decided to change his tactic. A few days later, the guard at the fence informed Jeab and his crew that the town's leader had permitted only one person to come in with a camera, no communication devices and no recordings.

'Fine. It's better than nothing.' Jeab and his crew accepted the offer. He gave his cell phone and video camera to the guard, leaving his team outside. Once he walked past the archway to the sacred land, the town's residents greeted him—men or women, young or old, everyone had a smile on their face. They were all farmers, dirty and skinny, but everyone praised the Lord and Father's compassion constantly, no matter how much Jeab questioned them.

'I'd like to meet the head of the village,' he said.

'Father's busy today. He'll dine with you tomorrow evening. Please rest for the night,' a female disciple replied with a deep bow.

Jeab was thoroughly pampered inside the house that the disciples had prepared for him. Early morning on the next day, he received a basket full of newly harvested fruits and freshly brewed coffee from the locals. In the afternoon, the disciples took him out into the field to savour the cool, fresh air and watch the cattle being herded while appreciating the view of the distant sea. Every meal was simple yet flavourful. No matter where he went, the villagers would smile and politely wave at him, saying 'God bless you.'

In the evening, he sat at the dining table with Father. The cool and composed middle-aged man whom he was meeting for the first time, invited him to listen to 'That Cause Can Never Be Lost Nor Stayed'. Father's eleven little angels sang the hymn along with the piano. As if in the firmament of a golden dream, the air was glowing, the lights shining bright, the hours snipped off and suspended in time, and he, lost in a daze, forgetting why he was even there. He would have been able to leave safely if he had not received a paper star from a darling Little Lamb who curtsied in front of him. When he unwrapped the star, it revealed a small message written in pencil that read: 'I've been kidnapped. Help me.'

Jeab immediately snapped out of the golden dream. He and his crew had investigated a rumour that this strange town had somehow been linked to a decade-long case of children's disappearances before. It occurred to him now that a lot of the kids and their parents here didn't share much resemblance. This seed of suspicion made him want to go back and recheck the information about the children who had vanished in public without a trace, years ago. Unfortunately, this journalist was too hasty. When he asked to meet Father in the middle of the night before leaving, Father noticed his agitation.

The man never made it out of that room.

At dawn, the disciples informed everyone that the outsiders had left in the bronze van. Everything returned to normal. Father sat down for breakfast with his eleven Little Lambs as if nothing had happened. Fatima and Stella glanced at each other. They'd hung their hope by a thread, not knowing that the thread had been severed the previous night.

That afternoon, an announcement from the town's speakers told the people to gather at the meeting room after dinner because tonight the church would hold a special ritual called the Sacred Night. The disciples herded the unsuspecting townspeople away from their homes, even the elders and infants. Whispers echoed off the walls. Everyone had heard of the Sacred Night before. It was a doctrine Father mentioned when he taught about the Book of Revelation and the Apocalypse. The seven angels blew their trumpets and set innumerable disasters upon land and waters. Father said in his enchanting voice that once the Sacred Night arrived, everyone inside the Holy Fences would leave together for the Kingdom of Heaven. And tonight was the night.

According to the record of the Messenger named Vikal, he was sent here to play a great farewell ensemble with ten other

Messengers, and the occasion was marked as the grandest string ensemble in years. The Messengers watched the people in the meeting room pass cups of poisonous cocktails to each other. Parents fed their children first and the elders were next. After that, students, labourers, the Little Lambs, the disciples, and Father, in that sequence. Fatima and Stella, whose hearts were still hanging onto a thread of hope, hadn't expected this pitiful end. They held each other's hand, watching the children and the elders drop to the floor one by one, writhing in pain. Once it was Stella's turn, the remaining villagers all turned to stare at her, a walking angel among them. She raised the wine glass with both hands, a breathtaking image. Before the first drop of liquid fell on her lips, however, Fatima, who was standing at the end of the line, rushed toward Stella and slapped the glass out of her hands. Shards of broken glass mixed with the dark liquid on the floor.

'Let's run!' he shouted and pulled Stella's hand.

At that moment, the crowd dispersed. The scene awoke in the people who had just drunk the poison, the sudden but inherent human instinct to stay alive. They abandoned the ritual and started screaming. The ones at the back slammed themselves against the padlocked doors. Father stood behind the pulpit. Having predicted that this would happen, he'd ordered the loyal disciples to close off all the exits and slit the throat of the Little Lamb who wouldn't drink the poison. Some of the Lambs were terrified enough to drain their cups immediately, the foul smell of urine penetrating the air. Veiled by chaos, Fatima took the chance to smash a small window open with a chair. He pushed Stella through the small opening and took her away from the meeting room. However, not long after, the disciples and the townspeople all swarmed out of the room like ants.

Both kids knew that the front gate was heavily bolted, so they quickly found themselves a hiding spot and waited for the commotion to die down. The first place that Stella thought of was the hollow of the rain tree that she always ran away to whenever she wanted to cry alone at night. They pushed themselves into the hollow, closing their eyes and ears to the horror outside. The screams and pleas of people who were being hunted down by the disciples as they climbed over the barbed wire fence. Fatima sat near the opening of the hollow. He knew full well that Father's men were looking for him and Stella. Heavy footsteps moved closer and closer.

'Wait here.' He stood up. A soft cry slipped out of Stella as she grabbed his arm. 'Stay here and, please, listen to me. We must part for only a moment. I'll draw them away. You must stay here. Do you understand?'

'I'm not letting you go anywhere!' She yanked at his clothes. 'We'll get out of this place together. If you die here, I will, too.'

Fatima found that his heart was incredibly calm when he looked at the determination on her face. He nodded, more certain than ever about the path he'd take.

'I'll be back, I promise. You mustn't move an inch. Even if you're hungry or if your stomach hurts, you mustn't make a sound. Wait for me.'

The girl stared at him before letting go of his shirt. He kissed her forehead softly and dashed out of the hollow like a wild hare. An armed disciple spotted Fatima and ran toward him instead. Fatima spent almost an hour trying to lose him. Once he had the time to catch his breath, Fatima took in his surroundings. Lying on the ground in hundreds, were corpses.

The apocalypse was in front of him. Bodies piled in pools of vomit. Tendrils of smoke rose up from the church and the hall. Father and the rest of the disciples had drunk the poison and burned down the den of evil with themselves in it. A flock of nocturnal birds had taken over the sky.

It's over, Fatima thought. *It's really over.* He quickly returned to the rain tree where he'd left his best friend. 'Stella,' he called. She was lying there, stiff. 'Wake up. Let's get out of here.'

But the girl didn't move. When Fatima took a closer look, he saw that her lips had turned purple, blood and saliva frothing from the corner of the mouth. Her eyes were wide open.

She had been killed by another disciple, the man who'd left his water buckets and ran to her when she'd fallen from the rain tree the first time. He knew that the tree would be the first place she would come and hide. Though when he saw her face, he didn't want blood to dirty this porcelain doll that God had created, so he forced her to drink a whole bottle of poison before running away to die with his fellows and his beloved leader, not waiting to watch the girl's final moments. Everything had happened while Fatima was playing hide-and-seek with another killer in the woods.

Fatima hugged Stella's soulless body, crying like a dying swan the same way he'd done when he'd been born. He kept calling her name, trying to wake her up, telling her to stop pretending to be asleep and get up. He carried her on his back and walked to the barbed wire fence. On the ground in front of it were the bodies of people who had been poisoned but still tried to climb over the fence just to drop down like fallen leaves. He hopelessly shook the lock several times before deciding to take her back to the rain tree. Fatima sat beside her cold body, apologizing for not being able to save her as promised and cursing her for leaving him. 'It was you who should have been alive,' he muttered. 'Not me.'

After a marathon of farewell songs the entire night, Vikal stopped in front of the hollow and studied the children who were on his list of the dead. Stella's spirit looked up at him from inside the hollow. She stroked Fatima's white hair, the boy unconscious from exhaustion after an entire night of running and crying. The girl smiled at Death, fearless.

She said, 'Please take him with you.'

Vikal didn't accept or refuse. Once he sent her away with his requiem, the boy next to her opened his eyes and stared at Vikal, terrified. He let the boy scream and scratch his fingers bloody, trying to make his way deeper into the hollow. When the boy exhausted himself and gave up, Vikal offered him his hand.

The Messenger asked for his name, even though he already knew.

The boy said his name was Stella.

22

'Jewels of the Madonna'

At this hour, the world of the living is bathed in bright silver light. Nocturnal birds are sleeping. Old wooden doors shriek in the silent rooms. Even if I try to walk as lightly as a cat, Vikal will open his eyes as soon as I open the door. The curtains in our room are pulled closed, darkness thick and unmoving. He lies in bed under a blanket, facing the wall. He must have realized that I already talked to the barn owl and learned about the things that he didn't want to explain himself. I sit on the floor next to his bed and whisper that I have remembered everything.

'Everything?' Vikal murmurs.

'Everything,' I reply softly. 'Once I remembered the important part, everything started to come back.'

Vikal goes silent and doesn't say anything else. I tug at his blanket, asking to be let in next to him. He shifts, giving me the space. When I put my head against his back, he says that it's too hot. 'You're big. Go sleep in your own bed,' he complains. I reach out my hand and intertwine my fingers between his, begging him to let me stay like this for a while. I can barely find the strength to stand on my own feet, the waves of memories rushing in all at once. Vikal doesn't say anything. Kind, gentle Vikal, always willing to be taken advantage of.

'Tell me about the beginning, when you first took me in.'

Vikal thinks about it for a while before letting out a sigh.

'After telling me that your name is Stella, you didn't say anything else for almost a year. You didn't care about the outside world, only standing there like an unfeeling doll. At mealtime, you sat still with a spoon in your hand, but you never touched the food. At bedtime, you lay there with your eyes open. When you fell asleep, you cried yourself awake from the nightmares. I thought you were done for,' he talks slowly, a clear note of mercy in his low, hoarse voice. 'I taught you how to write and read again. I told you stories every day. But I'm a Messenger, I don't know any good stories of the living. I had to beg the owner of the bookshop to find me good children's books. That man only gave me scary books about ghosts and monsters, but even so, you ate up every word, every line. I think it was only then that I saw the light in your eyes.'

For almost three years, I closed off my heart from the outside world, spending each passing day and night searching for Stella in my memories. In a parallel timeline, Vikal tried his best to gather the pieces of a broken child even when there was no way of knowing if he was going to succeed.

'I really troubled you a lot.'

When I say that, he scolds me and says that I am being ridiculous.

'The living always move forward,' Vikal says. 'The dead own the past. The Messengers own nothing. You're still alive. Past flows inside you, present courses through your limbs, future lies ahead, endless. Please realize how important life is.'

I ask him if this is the reason he never called me Stella or even by my real name. For me to keep living even if I had to trick myself with an alternative identity. And for Stella to stay alive in my mind forever.

'Carrying the fallen world of two kids at the same time. You're being too harsh on yourself, Vikal.'

Vikal's hands are damp and trembling slightly.

'That girl wanted you to be happy.'

I laugh. 'What about you?'

He turns back to stare at me.

'I want the same thing, Fatima.' Vikal's eyes never leave mine. 'Please keep on living.'

That sentence contains three-tenths of hope, while the rest is fear and resignation toward the fate that's already been written. I will die in the tower in the next few hours because I have been involved with Babel and the serial killer. Vikal wants to keep me here. He wants this life that he has saved, to grow up, to live and to have a happy future.

Future?

What kind of future has Vikal pictured for me? I have never thought about my own future. Since birth, I was pushed here and there by Mom's will. I had to study the Bible and practise chorus as Father commanded. I got to meet Stella, an extraordinary girl from the other side of the fence. When I saw her tears, I wanted to take her away from that hellhole. I wanted her to live, to hold my hand in the sea, to climb every tree out there and to be a princess of a faraway land somewhere.

I failed to protect her.

Stella is gone. She is nowhere in the world anymore.

If you ask me what I see in my future, right now, there's only one thing.

I want to help that girl.

After pestering Vikal and the bat hawk with the non-stop pleas, I finally get to tag along with the team of four Messengers back to the tower before sunset. On the outside, nothing changes. The wrought iron gate is still unlocked. The ground is covered with dust, puddles of sewage water, climbing figs, moss, and mould, which is also gobbling up the walls, from the cement surfaces to the steel frames inside. What feels weird is the atmosphere. It was already gloomy before, but now it feels sad and dejected enough to collapse from a single gust of wind. I look at my old home with longing. The tower of nightmare has been completely possessed by a demon—the demon whom I gave a name.

The bat hawk draws a circle on the ground around the tower. She, Vikal, the barn owl, and the fish owl—each of them assumes a position in a direction around the circle. 'String Quartet is the most efficient position for demon cleansing,' Vikal explains while holding his violin at the ready. 'We'll play the first note together when the demon appears. It'll be restrained inside the tower, unable to strike back like last time. But there are two disadvantages. First, before the song is over, the Messengers can't move from their positions . . .'

'What about the second one?' I ask.

'The demon already knows about the trespassers. It may not appear for the entire night. That's why a decoy is very crucial. No demons can withstand the scent of a delectable meal in front of them, and their most favourite meal in the world is a human's hopelessness before their last breath.'

Vikal swallows and looks at me with worry.

'. . . Do you hate me?'

Vikal's troubled expression makes my heart race. I stare into his eyes, forgetting myself, not knowing if it's because I'm touched by his honest confession that he's scared of being hated by me or because I am anxious about what I'm about to do. I wait until the last glimpse of the sun fades away, looking at the glowing circle under Vikal's feet. It prevents him from going away.

I say, 'I don't hate you, because I never meant to sacrifice that kid to the murderer in the first place.'

I beam. Vikal widens his eyes. He finally understands why I asked to come here.

'But no matter what, I don't think I can hate someone as gentle as you. Thank you for saving me. Goodbye.'

Vikal's lips twist. 'Don't say it if you're going to die!' he shouts after me when I start to run up the stairs to the theatre on the eleventh floor. He must want to stop me, but it's too late. He cannot step away from the circle.

'I love you, Vikal.'

I shout without looking back at him.

It is a shame that I can't see his expression right now.

23

'Serenade'

'Twinkle, twinkle, Little Star . . .'

'Parva Stella, tell us a story.'

'Ah, you're still as noisy as ever.'

I receive a warm welcome from the Lost Ones. The leader celebrates by making me a crown out of dry grass and putting it on my head, after which he chants, 'unga-bunga-bunga' while running in circles around me. Four Eyes and Shorty grab my shirt and pretend to cry (lies), begging me not to leave them again. Three girls clasp their hands together and whistle, 'coo-coo' imitating a dove, as a welcome for me. The rest cling to my legs, asking for a new story from me, their voices filling the stairwell. My heart is full. I am finally back home.

'Not now, rascals,' I say. 'Make way. I have something important to attend to in my old bedroom.'

They stick to me like gum. I don't have a choice except to go into the theatre with them, all ten of us. When I open the door, I am hit with a wave of dust that's been accumulating for a while because no one comes here to clean anymore.

I cough, covering my mouth. It looks like a hundred years have passed in the theatre on the eleventh floor. In the sea of dust, the teal curtains are bunched up on the floor full of glinting crystal beads. The plants in the boneyard are all dried up.

The Gambler's fragile bones are scattered to every corner by the wind. The Lost Ones and I march inside past all the obstacles, to the dressing room, the place where Babel used to rummage through my closet and throw dozens of my velvet dresses on the floor, right next to the pieces of torn ribbons. I look at the clothes. It hasn't been long, yet I cannot imagine my tall body in those dresses that 'Stella' would have loved to wear, anymore.

'You're here, right?' I crouch down and whisper to a pile of clothes. 'Babel?'

The pile of clothes is silent. Even the rowdy children feel the need to quiet down because of it.

'Hide all you want. I know you're here. I named you.'

I poke at the white dress with an embroidered rabbit.

'You're probably afraid that I'm here as a decoy. Never mind, just listen to me then. Tonight, four Messengers are here for you. Your beloved serial killer will murder another kid here. Everything has been planned to the T to take care of you. And you can't really choose not to eat the food that's handed to you on a silver platter, can you?'

'Wait, Stella, what are you talking about?' Shorty interrupts.

'That man's coming? I'm scared,' Four Eyes whines.

'Twinkle, twinkle, Little Star. Parva Stella, let's play Simon Says,' Pinkie cries.

'Let's play musical chairs,' Freckles shouts.

The younger ones harmonize, 'Let's play, let's play.'

'Shhh . . .' I admonish, but the kids don't stop their pestering. Not surprising, considering that this serial killer is the one who took their lives, the person the Lost Ones fear the most even in the afterlife. Every time he appears at this tower, the children cannot stay still. They run around and rush to me for more stories to soothe their grief and escape the reality of their deaths. This time, they are trying to do the same thing.

But not anymore.

I will not let it happen again.

'Lost Ones.' I climb onto the padded chair and announce, 'I, as the new leader of the Lost Ones at this tower, I think it's time for us to . . .'

'What are you saying, Stella?' Freckles complains. 'I'm the leader of the Lost Ones. Everyone! Stella isn't one of us. Stella is becoming an adult, and we hate adults very much, right?'

'Yes,' the lackeys harmonize. 'We hate adults.'

'So, we should chase Stella away before he becomes an adult.'

'Yes,' they say and frown. 'Um, no.'

The kids look at each other, confused, torn between whether or not to chase me away. I see a chance to intervene.

'I know that you all hate adults. That's why we have to work together and get rid of our common enemy first: an adult.'

I put my hands on my waist. Everyone turns to stare at me, including Babel. I can feel it eavesdropping from the pile of clothes.

'The man who's coming here tonight is the one who killed you all. He's brutal. He's our true enemy. Lost Ones, if you keep running away, more and more Lost Ones will be killed. If he's not caught, your parents will never find you. Don't you want to meet your parents?'

'I do,' the kids whisper, light as a feather, more fearful than anything else. But that is enough. Everyone starts to ask each other, 'What should we do now?'

I say, 'We'll get that man and save the kid. I can't do it alone. I need your courage and a little help from a certain someone who's been listening to us.'

I point to the pile of clothes that has backed up against the wall. A murmur of surprise erupts when the children see the clothes move, forming a question mark on the wall. Babel has been listening to us. The dressing room's floor trembles minutely. A voice resonates in my head. It's talking to me through telepathy.

Interesting. Explain.

'I want you to stay still.' I force a smile. 'You'll let the kid go. You won't protect the killer.'

Eh . . ?

It drawls, pretending to be confused.

What will I get in return?

I touch a finger to my lips.

'What's more delicious than the final scream of a human?'

The negotiation is a success after I describe the plan to Babel. The demon promises that it will cooperate and I promise that I will give something to it in exchange. *Does this mean I have made a deal with a demon?* I feel a little uneasy inside. What happens to a spirit that cuts a deal with a demon? Father used to say, 'If humans welcome Satan's seduction, they will not be welcomed into the Kingdom of Heaven.' Even though those words came out of the mouth of a hypocrite, the idea is still stuck inside my head. If I died here, would I still be able to hear Vikal's farewell tune? I lean out of the window and look at Vikal, who's standing at his post on the circle. He's there, seeming irritated and anxious, yet still holding onto the Messengers' rule. I only hope that he'll continue to do so, because if he disobeys a Senior Messenger's order by dashing after me, everything will fall apart. And he'll do that if he comes to know what I have promised Babel.

It is twelve past nine, according to the pocket watch. Babel says directly into my mind that the man has arrived at the tower. He doesn't come in through the wrought iron gate at the front, of course. He enters through the deserted road connected to a small canal at the back. I watch him from behind a pole, feeling hot and cold as if I'm about to catch a flu, when I lay my eyes on him for the first time. He's a man with a big frame, kind-looking and younger than I expected. The Lost Ones told me that he smelled bad. I cannot smell him from here, but I can sense the same aura as Father when he tried to kiss my cheek. Disgusting like rotten garbage full of maggots. I blink repeatedly to chase the feeling away.

A quarter past nine. He carries a sack all the way to one corner of the tower on the ground floor. I always thought that the vibration in the wall came from the floors above the theatre. That is why when I ran around looking for him all over the tower, I was only met with disappointment. I follow him. He has been hiding the kids right under our noses. The ground floor where the Lost Ones run past every night. A mere hundred metres away from the Gamblers' courtyard. This man is not a competent serial killer. Without Babel's illusion, his sloppy traces have become clear as day.

Twenty past nine. Three or four pairs of footsteps can be heard within the tower. The sound reaches the young man's ears and he halts. The man looks to his left and his right. *His heart is beating so fast, my dear Stella,* Babel talks to me. *When will you make a move?* it prompts. I scoff, *A bit longer. I'm waiting for an opening.*

Just a small one is enough.

The moment when he glances away from his prey.

Twenty-three past nine. Noises erupt from every direction. Hands drumming on buckets. Nails scratching the walls. Everything is the Lost Ones' expertise. I order the kids to move closer and closer to the target. The killer's face starts to pale. He puts the sack down, looking around as if he's about to run away. I smile. Babel whispers in my head, *It's not as easy as you think. He'll kill the kid. The girl's already seen his face.*

And that he does. He opens the sack. Young, little Pafhun, seven years old, with a ball of rags in her mouth, arms and legs firmly bound. She's still breathing, but it's a shallow thing. Severe bruises bloom all over her body. Realizing that he doesn't have the time to stuff her inside the wall like the other kids, the man takes out his knife, the blade shining in the dim light. The second he raises the weapon, he notices a reflection of me standing behind him.

The man is startled and immediately lets go of his victim. The same moment, I give the demon an order.

Babel, conceal her.

The girl and the sack instantly vanish. Babel can use an illusion to hide her but can't take the girl away from the tower because that will make the Messengers begin their cleansing ritual at once. And so, the rest of the duty falls on us. I look into the eyes of the confounded killer, saying, 'Found you!' I then turn around and run away into the darkness.

The killer knows what this means. Somebody has seen him. A living person has seen him. He forgets both his fear and the fact that he hasn't killed his victim, and chases after me with his knife, like a wild dog. This situation reminds me of the Sacred Night behind the Holy Fences. That night as well, I was chased with a knife like this. I kind of miss it. I laugh. Babel asks if there's anything so funny. I say that he will see it soon.

I run up to the second floor, the third floor, the fourth floor. The killer stays on my tail the whole time. The distance between me and him becomes shorter and shorter. The eighth floor, the ninth floor. I didn't think I would lose to an outsider who's unfamiliar with the plan of the tower, but in reality, I am at a complete disadvantage because of how steep and dark the stairs are. From this angle, Vikal sees the chase happening in front of him, each round superimposing on top of each other. Worry appears on his face. I know what he is about to do.

'Don't you dare move an inch!' I shout at the top of my lungs, uncaring of what the killer will think. The person whom I want to stop is not him. 'I'm begging you, Vikal.'

I do not know if Vikal will do what I asked, but I can only believe in him.

The killer finally catches up to me on the eleventh floor. He grabs my long hair and drags me toward him before stabbing me in the middle of my torso. I fall onto the floor. He yanks the knife out and stabs me again in the same spot. I can feel the blade leaving me a few more times before everything goes numb. It's as if my body cuts off all my feelings so that I can still remain conscious through it.

The killer stares at me. I stare at him from the floor. He's dripping with sweat, pupils dilating.

'Who's Vikal?'

He snarls at me. When I spit onto the floor as an answer, the man kicks me in the stomach.

'Who were you with? Who else is here? Answer me now.'

What a laughable image. He reminds me of Father again, so I laugh, the sound tinged with the bitterness of my own blood.

'Why the fuck are you laughing?' he sputters.

I think about what Babel once said, about how this tower was like a whale's carcass a thousand metres under the sea surface. A small but rich ecosystem where the small critters eat off the carcass and the big critters consume the smaller ones. I look up, seeing all ten of the Lost Ones in a circle around us, hands intertwined. They look down at me, emotionless. Suddenly, the young man screams, and the weight that presses me to the floor disappears. He sees the kids, too.

'Leader.' I look into Freckles' eyes. 'What do you wanna play tonight?'

'Kabaddi,' Freckles replies curtly.

I smile. 'Good. Let's start.'

All ten kids begin to continuously chant, 'Kabaddi, kabaddi, kabaddi,' while darting at the young man. His face pales. He remembers all the sweet kids that he's buried inside the wall with his own hands. The kids also remember him very well. Without the power of the demon to protect him, this murderer doesn't seem as frightening anymore. As the children corner him, the man hopelessly crawls backward, away from them, with his tail tucked between his legs.

The rule of Kabaddi states that the game ends when the raider runs out of breath to keep saying 'kabaddi'. But these kids aren't humans. They do not breathe. So, the chant—kabaddi, kabaddi, kabaddi—goes on, unending. The Lost Ones seize each of the killer's limbs as if they are worker ants carrying a carcass back to their colony. They start to sing the song that they have been singing every evening.

'Twinkle, twinkle, Little Star,

How I wonder what you are . . .'

The children stop at the edge of the tower. The wind brushes against them.

'Up above the world so high,

Like a diamond in the sky . . .'

The man screams and begs for his life. I finally realized how the killer felt. I drink in the enemy's final cry right before he takes his last breath. The happiness that has been brewing for a long time ripens at the moment of revenge. The children let his body go at the window. The man becomes just another star that falls down to the courtyard in front of the tower.

The image before me is fading, as is my breath. I'm happy that I succeeded. Babel is still staring at me from the wall. I promised it a delectable meal, and that is definitely not a killer's despair, which was only an appetizer. The best meal should supply the demon with power. Power that will give it enough strength and confidence to take down four Messengers at the same time.

'Take it, Babel.'

I look at it.

'My memories, my future, I give them all to you.'

It is a dying man's hope to stay alive.

Babel beams cheerily from the wall.

I will leave the rest to you, Vikal.

24

'Death and the Maiden'

What are you practising?

'Death and The Maiden.'

This piece was originally performed by a string quartet. Quartet means there are four musical instruments. Have you heard of it before?

Nope.

Doesn't matter. Just imagine it.

All four instruments have to play the first note at the same time. This piece needs two violins, one viola, and one cello, all of them seizing the attention of the audience since the very first verse. This bright and fast tempo is called allegro. After that, the four instruments start to fight, the melodies layering, harmonizing, and destroying one another all at once . . .

As soon as Babel opens its mouth to devour his gourmet meal, its body appears before the four Messengers. They have been standing with their instruments at the ready for hours. Once they sense a vibration from the tower, they rake the bow against their strings almost at the same time. The strategy that they have been practising all night long isn't exactly off to a good start, thanks to the fish owl, who accidentally nodded off on the circle while waiting. When he startles awake, the others are already playing the third bar.

The demon expands in an instant. Vikal sees two arms and two legs sprouting from the tower, bold and uncaring of the farewell ritual. Once it flicks its arm, a gust of wind blows all the curious nocturnal birds off the swaying wires and into the side of the building opposite from the tower, their small bodies dropping onto the street below. Vikal suspects from the very beginning that the food that the demon swallowed must not be something as mundane as fear or sorrow. He doesn't want to guess what it is. The ritual requires his undivided attention right now.

The air around them is warped. Black clouds gather above the tower in one spot. Babel fuses itself with weeds on the ground, using them as appendages to expand its territory. A climbing fig springs up around the barn owl's leg and pulls her down. All at once, the circle snaps apart like a worn rubber band. The vines begin their attack on the fish owl by dragging him inside the tower. Vikal sees him letting go of his viola, howling.

'Chief,' Vikal calls.

'The string quartet isn't powerful enough to stop it!' the Senior Messenger says. She screeches, a calling signal to all the nocturnal birds in the area. The demon cleansing ritual is a dangerous ceremony. Nobody wants to be involved without a specific order. The other Messengers reluctantly show up on the other side of the road and improvise along with their own instruments. Even Vikal, who has the patience of a saint, feels like his ears are going to explode from these unsynchronized melodies.

Babel continues flaunting its attacks for some time. At one point, it starts to feel the scorching pain growing from below. It discovers that among this chaos of the terrible tunes, there's one melody that is killing it slowly from the inside. It's the wild and aggressive bowing from Vikal who is standing there, facing the demon, unafraid. In that moment, he stares into its eyes, and inside he sees the spirit and memories of Fatima wavering there. The demon realizes too late that Vikal isn't playing this piece for it, but for that kid. And that kid reacts by burning himself down with a smile.

It's so beautiful, Vikal.

Babel hears Fatima from the inside. It shrieks a final enraged cry, swinging its arms around and bringing many Messengers down with it as it burns, leaving horrendous black mucus on the walls. The bat hawk leads the team inside to inspect the aftermath before announcing officially that the cleansing ritual is now complete.

They carry the wounded fish owl away. The barn owl and the rest of the Messengers leave after such an exhausting night. In the shining light of the new morning, Vikal is still there in the tower, looking for Fatima amid the dark goo. He eventually finds Fatima's soulless body in a pool of blood on the eleventh floor. The boy is dead. Stabbed. Multiple times. Vikal cries quietly. Sorry that he didn't even have the chance to play a farewell melody for the spirit of the boy he raised. Regret that he hid many important things from him. No time even to respond to the boy's last wish.

Vikal blinks away his last tear when he hears the stumbling footsteps from behind.

'Ah, you're here.' The bat hawk stops next to him, a cane in her hand. He quickly wipes away any wetness from his face and bows. 'No, no, relax. When I said, "you're here", I didn't mean you.' The Senior Messenger cackles. Her eyes are on the black goo on the wall. She rolls up her sleeves and sticks her hand into the viscous sludge oozing an evil aura.

'Vikal, do you know what we were before we became Messengers?'

Vikal raises an eyebrow, replying, 'No, ma'am.'

'Humans.' She smiles. 'Humans who made a deal with demons. When a demon is cleansed, the human spirit inside them will be, too. That's why we have to work our asses off to make up for it. Until we get promoted to Senior Messenger—only then can we retire whenever we want. That's when we can finally move on, like the others.'

The bat hawk pulls her hand back from the dark mucus, something round and milky white inside it. She offers it to Vikal. In her hand is a cute little egg.

'It seems like this boy is a cockatoo.' The bat hawk sounds thrilled. 'Not a nocturnal bird, but I guess it doesn't hurt to have something unusual once in a while.'

Vikal widens his eyes.

'Is that him?'

'Yes.'

'May I see him?'

Actually, Vikal wants to say, 'May I take care of him?' But he knows that the Chief will definitely refuse. And he is right. She doesn't even let him touch the egg. 'Not now, Vikal,' the Senior Messenger says. 'The recovered spirit egg must be hatched at the office. But,' her voice sweetens once she notices the sad tilt of his lips, 'don't worry, you'll get to teach him.'

'Huh?'

'As his senior . . .'

She then transforms back into the bat hawk and flies away with the cockatoo egg that will become Messenger Fatima in the near future.

In the world of the living, the next morning, the local who walks the path in front of the tower every day finds a grisly scene behind the wrought iron fence. The body is identified as a man in his early thirties who worked as a primary school teacher. Later, he is identified as the notorious serial killer, according to the statement given by seven-year-old Pafhun, who miraculously survived.

The police find her curled up in pain inside a sack while they are investigating the crime scene. They send her to the hospital and return her to her parents' care. The girl remembers everything about the abduction and the culprit's appearance, down to the last detail. When shown some photos, she can also tell him apart from the other suspects. However, what surprises the adults the most is her words after that.

'The leader of the Lost Ones asked me to tell everyone this: "Please take us home too."'

She tells them that when the wounds hurt too much and she thought she was going to die, she saw kids her age sitting around her in a circle. They reached out and touched her wounds, and the wounds began to hurt less. They stayed with her until morning, telling her a story. One about a beautiful mermaid with hair twinkling like stars and eyes the same colour as the sea . . .

After that, the police conduct a major excavation within the tower's area, which leads to the Lost Ones finally reuniting with their families. The barn owl tells Vikal that she is the one who sent their spirits away.

'They were good kids. When I played "Twinkle, twinkle, Little Star", as requested, they held hands and danced around me. It was so adorable.'

'Their babysitter would be happy to know that,' Vikal replies.

'Who?'

He says 'nothing' before holding out his hand for a cigarette. Two plumes of smoke linger in the filthy air in front of Ghostwalk Alley.

Even though almost everything has been solved and the city has gone back to how it was before, one mystery remains unanswered: the body of the white-haired boy that the rescue unit found at the tower on the eleventh floor. He lay in a dry pool of blood with his fingers intertwined. His eyes were closed, an angelic smile on his face. No one knows where the boy came from. He's unidentifiable. No documents can pinpoint who he was. An officer told the journalists that despite the state of disarray inside the theatre, there are traces that someone used to live there.

Internet users who love their conspiracy theories might enjoy this particular news, but the legal owner of the building doesn't. The owner of the tower is rather upset that there were trespassers who had been living inside the property that he's been trying to sell. He is afraid that vagrants and adrenaline junkies will come and settle down here, so he makes a sign that reads 'PRIVATE PROPERTY – NO TRESPASSING' and puts it up on the wrought iron fence, along with hiring 24x7 security to keep people from disturbing the peace of this forty-seven-storey tower.

But the owner can only forbid the living.

The Gamblers' parade still goes on like stars falling from the top floor every night, as well as the despair in the final moments of the young murderer's life, that lingers in the form of squiggly lumps of dust in the building's dark corners, waiting for someone to find and name it, so that one day it will become the next demon of this place.

It's a shame when it gets eaten by a wandering demon from afar who is looking for a place to stay in the city.

'It's so noisy outside, but the inside looks pretty homey,' the demon mutters to himself while munching on the food. 'Oh well, this Mr Sparks will try not to cause any trouble, then.'

And the story of the people in the world after sunset goes on . . .

Epilogue: Romance

Andante

'Vikal.'

'Mhmm.'

'You always seem sad when you look at me. Why?'

'What kind of face am I making right now?'

'Like this.'

'I don't do that.'

'You're surprisingly a crybaby.'

'Just focus on your practice.'

I steal his kiss the first time we practise 'The Flower Duet' on our violins. Dawn is almost breaking. His hair is down and his glasses are off. A light breeze slips through the gaps in the window, making it seem like there's a black river flowing on the side of Vikal's face. The moment our lips meet, his eyes widen slightly, but there is no resistance.

I ask him, 'Does it feel good?'

He nods.

After that, it seems like we keep on stealing each other's kisses everywhere.

Adagio

The bat hawk—a former Messenger who recently retired—told me that Vikal had volunteered to take care of me. I once asked him if there was any special reason, but he immediately changed the subject.

On the last day as a trainee, I tell Vikal I love him. When I hear him say 'you, too', I can't really believe my own ears. For the past three months that I have been following him as his junior, Vikal always looked at me with sadness in his eyes. Sometimes, he'd look away. When he gave me lessons, his voice would be shadowed by sorrow. But it's this grief he wears that makes me desire him more and more every day. All the little things about him: his tightly pressed lips, the fine hair beside his ears, thick lashes under the lenses of his glasses, his pale, translucent skin, the tall, wiry frame. He is especially ticked off when he has to look up while talking to me. One time, I heard him talk in his sleep, 'You were so little before . . .' and when I ask him who he meant, he feigned ignorance.

'I'm serious, Vikal. Who's it? Your ex-lover?'

'Do not press me.'

'I'm jealous.'

'Hmph.' He covers his mouth and laughs.

'What?'

'Nothing.'

Vikal must not realize that he is smiling. The corners of his lips curve up slightly behind his hair that gleams in the dim light. The picture almost makes me forget how to breathe.

'Staring into beauty is no different from staring Death in the eye.'

'What are you talking about?' Vikal rests his chin on the ledge of a window in this deserted house. 'Where did you learn something that cheesy?'

I do not know either. Sometimes strange words and unfamiliar actions just occur to me, and I am not able to recall where they're from. For example, immediately after we come home from our farewell duty, I lead Vikal to the chair and ask him to sit down, so that I can comb his hair from behind with a wooden brush. I don't know why I want to do this, but there is a word that often comes into my mind: gratitude.

Vikal seems shocked that I cut my hair short. Even though shoulder-length hair is usually regarded as long for men, he still can't keep his cool about it.

'You like long hair better?' I ask. He shakes his head.

A while after, I learn that he was just shy. It is then that I have a chance to tell him that I chose to be an independent Messenger instead of working for the authority, like him. Vikal does not object, and only asks about my reasons. I reply that my cockatoo form is too cute and fluffy to be the harbinger of Death. I want to travel the world and soothe the lost spirits I meet along the way. Once I finish my speech, I show him my white robe with yellow pattern that I bought during a sale from Ghostwalk Alley.

'See, Vikal. I look like a giant cockatoo in this.' I put the robe over my shoulders. Vikal crosses his arms and scrutinizes my latest fashion choice, before telling me that the pads on the shoulders look terrible.

'I'd rather burn it,' he quips.

Allegro

Not long after I start working, Vikal leaves the city.

The authority's Messengers have to move every four to five years, unlike the freelancers, who usually flock to the places that are full of illnesses, like the city. While Vikal is always busy, I only laze around here and there. Even though we're not joined at the hip like before, I still find several opportunities to go and visit him. Vikal writes to me saying that he has packed and is moving to stay at an old church in the west as instructed by the Senior Messenger. From his tone in the letter, it sounds as if he doesn't want me to visit him there. Even so, I stubbornly insist on helping him clean up the place.

The church that Vikal talks about is an old wooden structure, its white paint cracked and peeled by time. Next to the church is a meeting room that can accommodate up to around three hundred people, and from here, a deserted village on the hill can be seen. Vikal says that this village used to be an agricultural commune that was cut off from the outside world. Today, the town is uninhabited, but its ground is full of black stains and wriggly balls of howling dust demons.

'Something terrible happened here several years ago,' Vikal says.

'Where in the world have terrible things not happened?' I ask.

'You're right. But this place is worse than others. Any Messenger would tell you to stay away.'

Despite being the one who brought up the subject, Vikal refuses to go into more details. Sadness grips him again, so I tease that there must be nothing in the world that scares him and then change the subject. Vikal and I spend three days and three nights cleansing the lingering demons in the area. After that, we have some time to rest before going back to work.

I invite him to make love to me in the church, in a place that would later become his bedroom. I swear my love to him before a dark mahogany cross, slow and solemn. When I run my hands all over his body, Vikal squeezes his eyes shut and presses his lips against the soft moan that threatens to come out. I feel so guilty for not being able to stop, but both his arms are wrapped around my shoulders, hugging me close. Sometimes, I hear him murmur, 'Don't leave me again, please, don't go . . .' and then he presses kisses all over my temples. The care that he has for me is overflowing and from time to time, it makes me feel as if he is drowning in guilt and is trying to make up for it by being nice to me. A gesture that I wholeheartedly accept.

We spend the last day of our break at the beach, not far from the hill. Half of the moon gleams brightly above the water, turning the sea into liquid silver. Our feet step on the sea foam. The surrounding towns are sleeping. The wind rushes around us, producing a sound that resembles a weeping woman.

'Why does it have to be the sea?' I ask.

Vikal raises an eyebrow. 'You don't like it?'

'I do. Just didn't expect you to be the one to invite me here.'

Vikal stops walking. I stop, too, a few steps behind. He turns and looks me in the eyes.

'Fatima,' he calls me.

'Hmm?'

'Fatima.'

'Ah . . . yes?'

'How do you feel when your feet touch the sand?'

'Well,' I reply. 'Ticklish, I guess?'

'Ticklish?'

'Yeah, the sand sticks to my feet so I have to put in more effort when I walk. But it feels nice when the water rushes in and washes the sand off my feet.'

'Have you tried tasting the sea water?'

'You're acting weird tonight.'

Once I say that, Vikal halts and falls silent. I am a little confused. Vikal is weird. He doesn't really answer my questions when asked. After that, I invite him to sit on the beach, and Vikal sits down beside me without a word. Humming softly, I slowly untie his long hair, letting it drift in the wind like a black wave.

'You know, Vikal? There are mountains in the sea, too.'

I pull him in and let his head rest on my shoulder.

'Do you mean islands?'

'Islands are islands and mountains are mountains.' I laugh. 'Mountains in the sea aren't like the ones on land. They're not stable, not strong. They're small mountains that wobble around. Look, look, there they are.'

'Those are waves.' Vikal squints. 'Silly.'

'When the wind is calm and the air is clear, the mountains disappear and, in their place, we can see something else. The stars . . . the stars of the sun and the ones of the moon. There they are, on the face of the water, shimmering and glittering . . . Ah—'

Vikal looks up and asks if something is wrong.

'Vikal, you're crying.'

'I'm not crying.'

Vikal quickly wipes the tears away with his sleeve. I beam and pull him into a tight embrace.

Just as I thought. *Vikal really is gentle.*

Appendix

The compositions used as each chapter's title in the order of appearance:

1. 'Blackbird' (The Beatles, 1968)
2. 'Scene by the Brook, Symphony No. 6' (Ludwig van Beethoven, 1802–1808)
3. 'Flight of the Bumblebee' (Nikolai Rimsky-Korsakov, 1900)
4. 'Pathetique Symphony No. 6' (Pyotr Ilyich Tchaikovsky, 1893)
5. 'Partitas for Solo Violin' (Johann Paul von Westhoff, found in 1971)
6. 'The Flower Duet' (Léo Delibes, 1883)
7. 'The Devil's Trill' (Giuseppe Tartini, 1799)
8. '8 Humoresques, Op. 101' (Antonín Dvořák, 1894)
9. 'Traumerei', *Kinderszenen, Op. 15* (Robert Schumann, 1838)
10. 'Poème, Op. 25' (Ernest Chausson, 1896)
11. 'Passacaglia' (Heinrich Ignaz Franz Biber, 1606)
12. 'Sanctus' (Composer unknown) (a hymn from Christian liturgy)
13. 'From the New World, Symphony No. 9' (Antonín Dvořák, 1893)
14. 'Habanera', *Carmen* (Georges Bizet, 1875)
15. 'Dance of the Goblins' (Antonio Bazzini, 1852)
16. 'Ode to Joy', *Symphony No. 9* (Ludwig van Beethoven, 1824)

17. 'Gnossienne No. 1' (Erik Satie, 1893)
18. 'Spiegel im Spiegel' (Arvo Pärt, 1978)
19. 'La Campanella', *Grandes Etudes de Paganini, S.141* (Franz Liszt,1851)
20. *Orpheus and Eurydice* (Christoph Willibald Gluck, 1762)
21. 'Danse Macabre Op. 40' (Camille Saint-Saëns, 1874)
22. *Jewels of the Madonna*, (Ermanno Wolf-Ferrari, 1911)
23. *Serenade for Strings* (Antonín Dvořák, 1875)
24. 'Death and the Maiden', *String Quartet no. 14* (Franz Schubert, 1824)
25. *Romance in G Major* (Sergei Rachmaninoff, 1894)

Author's Note

It was as if everything was destined to begin on that day.

August 2019. I travelled to the capital city to visit a friend's office on Charoen Krung Road (the office that I borrowed and later adapted into Plerng's studio in *Blue Hour*). We watched movies until late at night, stayed the night there, and went out for breakfast together. On the way, she pointed at a creepy, abandoned building on Sathorn Road. 'Ghost building,' she said. 'Foreigners like to sneak in and take photos there. The owner doesn't allow it, actually, but you can still get in if you pay the guard.'

I started writing the first draft of *Death and the Maiden* in July 2020. My plan was that the protagonists would be a girl and Vikal, a chatty nocturnal bird who is also her imaginary friend. I wrote and rewrote three to four drafts, but once I got to around ten chapters, I had to take a break from the story to write *A Preyer at Sundown: Juveniles.* After that I continued with *Of Murder and the Muse* and then a *Share House* sequel, finishing two more books. Since I'd left *Death and the Maiden* and hadn't picked it up again in a long time, I didn't have any lingering ache for the book anymore, and the only thing left was a small amount of regret for the time I'd spent writing it. Until one particular vinyl record came into my possession around the end of February 2021.

Franz Schubert's 'Death and the Maiden', performed by Amadeus String Quartet.

My works have been influenced by classical music, forever and always, as if this brain and these hands are fuelled by fiery music. Schubert's 'Death and the Maiden' begins like a blazing flame. I cannot remember how I felt listening to the latter part of the piece, because Schubert and his symphony had stolen my heart ever since the very first note.

Death, a maiden, and the violin. This became the new theme of the book.

I changed the protagonist to a boy who wore skirts because I wanted to keep the 'original' protagonist to play an important role in the past of the story. When I explained the concept to Sarail, my partner, she didn't really understand the whole thing and assumed that I was going to write a corny, erotic story instead (dammit). Once she read the first four chapters, she thought it was going to be a dark detective story like *God Child.* I let her and the readers on the website *readAwrite* guess and wonder about the genre of the book until almost the end. Sarail confessed that my book wasn't really her cup of tea, but she still endured as my guinea pig reader, checking the rhythm, the sentences, and the logic of the story while I tried to magically pull everything out of thin air. It could be said that without her, I might have not made it. Therefore, everyone, please give her a round of applause. (Darling, if you're reading, I love you.)

Next is the topic of a secret town, a mysterious cult, and a radical belief.

I read about Jim Jones and the Jonestown Massacre from *Untitled Case: Human Horror* and a bizarre thought occurred to me. Combine that with the suppressed emotions throughout the six years of my all-girls boarding school (a place many Thai readers should be able to guess) and voilà! I spent my teenage years in that crazy school five days a week. I followed every rule even though I didn't understand it. I sang the worship songs, prayed, attended all the Bible classes, and then I grew up into a witch.

I think the products of my school aren't strict Christians, but witches! Confined by the rules that everyone had to follow, girls like us were burning with a longing for freedom and an identity that was locked up inside. Snacks hidden under duvet covers. Mobile phones inside shoe cabinets. Having surreptitious sex on bunk beds while the rest of the room pretended to be asleep. And so, the reasons for rebellion in a character like Stella—a girl born outside the fences—and Fatima—a boy who got pushed around so much that he never had a chance to dream about his own future—are completely different.

Vikal believes in humans' future; in the child he took in—that he'll be able to grow up and reintegrate into human society. It's a shame that both Fatima and I did not. I think that the faulty systems in our country, especially in the capital city, do not allow any mercy for homeless children who never exist anywhere. Fatima hasn't thought that far ahead, though. He only wants to make it up to Stella and repay Vikal's kindness.

My dear reader, you can assume that Fatima's love is unrequited when he's a human because he dies before hearing an answer. Vikal also comes to the same conclusion.

'Islands are islands and mountains are mountains. Mountains in the sea aren't like the ones on land. They're not stable, not strong. They're small mountains that wobble around. When the wind is calm and the air is clear, the mountains disappear and, in their place, we can see something else. The stars . . . the stars of the sun and the ones of the moon. There they are, on the face of the water, shimmering and glittering.'

In that moment, the picture that comes into Vikal's mind has a boy and a girl, hands held tight, running down the beach, stepping on mountains, tiny and wobbling. Their hands scoop up sunlight stars and moonlight stars, letting them fall through their fingers and down into the infinite water below.

He takes this kid to the sea.

But in the end, he is the one who cries.

Now, this cruel writer will reveal the truth about the novel that the reader is holding.

It is 'an album of photos of regrets'.

With love,
Apinuch 'Moonscape' Petcharapiracht, 2024